Bir

Also by Alison Prince:

Dear Del

Other Hodder titles you may enjoy:

Long Way from Chicago
Richard Peck

Law of the Wolf Tower
Tanith Lee

Silverwing
Kenneth Oppel

The Burning
Judy Allen

Bird Boy

ALISON PRINCE

Hodder
Children's
Books

a division of Hodder Headline

To Isabel, with love and thanks.

One

The black bird was staring in. Not just looking, but *staring*. It stood out there on the weedy terrace with its big claws firmly spread on the flagstones and its black beak thrust forward, and peered through the dirty glass of the tall French windows as if it really wanted to see who was inside.

Con stared back. Sunshine lay in long rectangles across the parquet floor of the huge room, and the cobwebbed velvet curtains smelt of dust. From the other side of the double doors that led into another room, just as big, he could hear his mother and father talking to the estate agent.

The bird had blue eyes, that was the extraordinary thing. Pale, brilliant blue. And it turned its head to fix first one blue eye then the other on the boy who stood inside the glass.

'What do you want?' asked Con.

But it didn't answer.

* * *

1

Look, look, the boy has come at last. Conan, the boy with my name. Only nobody called me by my name. They know me as Crow. Crow. Crow. The Bird Boy.

'I'm sure it's meant,' Arabella said that evening, as they sat round the kitchen table back in London. She pushed her hands through her dark hair and the sleeves of her purple patchwork shirt fell back from her arms. 'Don't you think so?'

'It's quite a coincidence, I'll give you that,' Neil agreed. 'But is it the right place to run a Yoga Centre? Stuck in the wilds of Suffolk? Wouldn't somewhere nearer London—'

'Neil, don't be so stuffy! It's exactly what people will want, all that peace and tranquillity, and even the name, Wilderness Hall – can't you see how perfect it is?'

Con glanced up from his maths homework and sighed faintly. What a noisy pair his parents were, always arguing and fussing, like a couple of budgies on a perch – specially his mother, with her bright black eyes and her brightly coloured clothes, as mad as parrot feathers.

Picking up his thoughts, Arabella said, 'Why don't you go upstairs, Con, if we're disturbing you? It's quieter in your bedroom.'

'No, I'm fine.' Con hated working in his bedroom

– it made him feel like an outcast. And anyway, this was too interesting to miss. Were they really going to buy the vast, shambolic place they'd been to see this afternoon? Mad, they were utterly mad. And what was this about being Meant?

'I never knew much about her,' Arabella was saying, 'just that her name was Larina and she was my gran's sister – the youngest, I think. They were a big family, the Bardinis. But I suppose my parents lost touch a bit after they came over here. This Larina caused a big scandal, anyway, because she went off with some Englishman she met in the mountains. She was only about sixteen. He was older. He'd come to Italy for his health. I expect he had TB – it was fashionable then.'

'But why elope with a man who had TB?' asked Neil. 'Not much of a future there.'

Arabella thought about it, chin in hand. 'Maybe that was the point,' she said. 'Maybe she wanted to fly away, see the world. And if he was going to die quite soon, she'd be free.'

'That's just your imagining of it,' said Neil.

'Yes, but she was my grandmother's sister,' Arabella pointed out. 'We're of the same blood. So of course I can imagine, because we're sort of joined. I know how she must have felt.'

'What are you talking about?' asked Con. 'And

3

what's all this got to do with the house?' He wished he hadn't gone to sleep in the car coming home – he'd obviously missed something. He'd been dreaming about the black bird. Dreaming it called him by his name, wanted to tell him something. Ridiculous.

'My great-aunt,' Arabella explained. 'Larina. This Englishman she married took her away to a place called Wilderness Hall. Oo-eel-dair-ness 'All.' She said the name again, in a strong Italian accent. Arabella had been born in London, but she was still very much a Bardini. 'I remember them talking about it,' she said. 'My dad took us to Lucca to see my gran, when I was quite small. We were sitting in this room with heavy lace curtains drawn against the heat of the afternoon, and I remember how that name stuck out from the rest of the conversation in Italian. I started repeating it, "Wilderness Hall, Wilderness Hall" because it sounded so funny – and got scolded for being rude, of course.'

'And that's the place we were at this afternoon?' Con was stunned. 'How weird! Or did you know about it?'

Arabella shook her head. 'I just saw the name in the advert. It absolutely jumped out at me. Then Mr Whatsit said—'

'Withers,' put in Neil. 'The estate agent.'

'Withers, OK – said the owner of the Hall had brought a young wife home from abroad somewhere,' Arabella rushed on. 'So that proves it, doesn't it?'

'Um, not really,' said Neil, who liked to get things right. 'There could be other Wilderness Halls. Other girls.'

'No, there couldn't. It sounded so right. The wild bride.' But then Arabella crumpled a little. 'Poor soul. She didn't find her freedom, did she? Not from what that snide little Withers said, implying she was batty. Anyone would think it's a crime to be non-English. And she died when she was still quite young. He said she committed suicide.' Arabella frowned. 'Isn't that awful? Poor Larina. I can't bear to think about it. And she had a son, too. I wonder what happened to him?'

The boy has come at last. Conan, the boy with my name. A prickle ran down Con's spine. 'What was his name?' he asked. 'The son's, I mean.'

'No idea,' said Neil. 'The main thing is, are we going to buy this place or not?'

Arabella smiled at him confidently. 'Of course we are,' she said. 'It's practically in the family, we *must*.' She leaned across the table and put her hand on Neil's shoulder.

'Darling, I do wish you'd learn to relax. Things

5

are never as scary as you think – you just have to stop fighting them.'

Neil shook his head wearily – but he'd given up arguing with Arabella's Yogic statements. '*You* just don't see the problems,' he said.

'What does Gran think?' Con enquired. 'After all, it's her money.' Aussie Gran, Neil's mother, had moved here from Sydney five years ago when her husband died, and she'd been doing the Lottery ever since. Never won more than a tenner on a scratch card until this February, then she'd been one of five people sharing the big one. Life at school had been pretty weird since then. People had kept asking Con for hand-outs. Kevin Tupp even had the cheek to say he needed a new computer.

'She's thrilled to bits,' said Arabella. 'We phoned her as soon as we got home. She's always wanted a place with a huge garden – you know what she's like.'

Con nodded. His gran worked in a garden centre in Croydon and complained that it was hopelessly small, even though there was miles of it. 'Will she come and live in the Hall?' he asked.

'Oh, yes, that's the whole idea. There's masses of room for a granny flat.' Arabella was alight with excitement. 'Poor house, it's been lost for all these years, but now it's found again.'

Con wondered how a place that size could get lost. Even an ordinary semi like the one they lived in now would be difficult to lose, though if you were absent-minded you might forget which one was yours, there being so many of them and so alike. But Wilderness Hall was something else. He should have gone into the estate agent's office with Neil and Arabella instead of shoving off to buy a can of Coke, but he didn't like the creepy little guy called Withers, and house-talk was boring. There'd been such a lot of it since Gran's win.

And anyway, there were other things to think about. Every time Con shut his eyes, he seemed to be standing again on the dusty floor of that big room, staring into the blue eyes of the crow or whatever it was. He saw it again now, against the background of his parents' voices, and said to it in the privacy of his mind, *I don't know what you want, but you'll have to wait.* And he saw the crow spread out its strong wings and lift off into the wide Suffolk sky.

I remember being a boy. The unwinged heaviness, the soft feet laced into shoes. The fear. It is so terrible to be ground-bound and denied the sky. When I saw my hands, I ran and ran. I tried to fly away from them. Conan, do you understand? Seeing is not just done with the eye – a day

7

comes when everything is newly real. So real that it hurts. All things are themselves, they need no names. And so I saw my human hands, thin-skinned and featherless. All wrong, all wrong.

Con woke, sweating. Stifled. He flung the duvet aside, and the clinging shreds of the dream made him expect to see not an arm but a bird's wing.

Stupid, he thought. Fighting his way to consciousness, he understood that he was in his own room and everything was normal. The cool, grey light of dawn was at the window, and all the birds of the suburban gardens were singing their praises of the coming day.

Two

Look, look. There he is again, standing in the long grass.
He had to come, he had to. Conan, Conan, you are
welcome.

Con stood behind the house, knee-deep in the
hayfield that had once been a lawn. The removal
van was round the front. People had kept telling
him not to get in the way, so he'd left them to it.
You'd have thought the baize-apron brigade would
appreciate a helping hand. Well, it was their loss.

Birds wheeled overhead. The dazzling autumn
sky was full of them, flying in wild circles round the
roofs and chimneys. Con wondered if the black crow
with the blue eyes was among them. 'You needn't
worry,' he said to them aloud. 'We haven't come to
disturb you. Just to live here.'

Anyone would think he was off his head, talking
to birds. Mad.

Mad. And with the word, a coldness came between
him and the sunshine. Why? Con rubbed first

one bare arm then the other, trying to dispel the gooseflesh that had bloomed on them so suddenly in the warm, late August day. Then he pushed his hands into his jeans pockets. The moment was somehow turning into a strange one, oddly intense.

So real that it hurts.

Where had he heard those words? Did he dream them?

'That's you moving in, then.'

The real, Suffolk-accented voice made Con jump with its closeness. He turned to find a girl standing behind him, and felt his face flush with furious embarrassment. What was she doing, creeping up on people like that? She must have heard what he said to the birds, too. She'd think he was nuts.

The girl was surveying him calmly, brown arms folded across her faded blue T-shirt. She had thick, untidy hair, as pale as the sun-bleached barley stubble in the fields.

'You from London?' she enquired. 'I saw the van go up the road. That had a London address on it.' Her voice had the heavy, laconic drag which seemed to speak of centuries of stone-picking and east wind.

'South London,' said Con. 'Penge.'

He could see this meant nothing to her. She shifted on her feet a little and asked, 'That right you won the Lottery?'

Con groaned inwardly. He'd hoped to move away from all that, leave it behind. How did people find out about these things? Must have been the estate agent, rat-faced little nark. 'My gran won it, actually,' he said. 'But she shared it with four other people, so it wasn't mega.' Nobody ever wanted to believe this, although it was the truth.

'That'll need to be mega if you're coming to live here,' the girl said flatly. 'The Hall's in a terrible state, they say.'

'Yes.' Wallpaper bulging away from the damp walls, loops of old-fashioned flex that didn't connect with anything, a dank kitchen where the light that filtered in through an ivy-covered window made the place look like a fish-tank. Changing the subject, Con asked, 'What about you? Where do you live?'

'At the farm.' She waved a casual hand, indicating somewhere beyond the row of elm trees. 'Wilderness Hall Farm,' she added, seeing his blank face. 'That's part of the estate.'

'What estate?'

She looked at him as if he was being stupid. 'Well, that's yours now. Used to be the Fothergills'. Mr Edwin first, then it shoulda bin his brother's, only he never rightly got it.'

'Why not?' asked Con.

The question fell into a sudden silence. Con

glanced round at the big house, and saw that the birds had settled on the roof in a dark crowd, as silent and attentive as if they were listening.

The girl looked at them, too, and when her eyes met Con's again she was frowning. 'They say there was bad things happened here,' she said. 'But you don't want to take no notice, not if you mean to stay in the Hall.'

'Oh, come *on*,' said Con with a flash of irritation. 'Nobody's afraid of stories. I'm just interested, that's all.'

She remained obstinately silent, staring away across the fields.

Con tried another tack. 'What's your name, anyway?'

'Maggie. Maggie Dew. What's yours?'

'Conan Bardini-Smith. They call me Con. What do people say about the Hall?'

Maggie shrugged. 'A lot of rubbish, most likely. But it's right there was this mad wife what run about talking to the birds. They was the only ones understood her, seemingly. They used to perch on her hands and that, people say. It got so she wouldn't come indoors, wanted to live wild like them.'

'What happened to her?'

'They put her away. Then she killed herself.'

They put her away. There was something dark about this, but Con had more urgent things to find out. 'The son – wasn't there a son?'

Maggie nodded. 'The Bird Boy. They say his name was Conan, same as yours. Funny, that. He were as mad as his mother.' She looked at Con from under her fringe of barley-pale hair and added, 'You bin doing a bit of asking, then?'

'Not really. It's just what the estate agent said.' Con was still kicking himself for not having taken more interest at the time.

'If that's Eric Withers, he'd know,' said Maggie. 'The Hall bin on their books for donkey's years.'

Voices drifted faintly from the front of the house. 'This in the master bedroom, sir?' 'Right, Bill, I've got it.' The birds still watched from the roof.

'They never found him,' Maggie said.

Con stared at her. 'Who? What d'you mean?'

'The Bird Boy. They waited years in case he came back. That's why the Hall was never on the market, 'cos it should have been his by rights. It's only these past few months they give up. There's a lot of people wanted it, but you was the ones with the cash.'

Find out. The two words were close and clear.

'But – what happened to him?' Con asked.

'Like I told you, nobody rightly know.' Maggie

turned away. 'I best be going. See you tomorrow, maybe.'

'Sure,' said Con. He felt faintly stunned.

Maggie looked back after a few paces through the long grass and said, 'If you want this ploughed and re-seeded, my dad could do it for you.'

'Right.'

This time, Maggie kept going until she disappeared into the overgrown shrubbery, beyond which was the line of elm trees and the open fields.

Ploughed and re-seeded, Con thought. He must tell Neil. It was going to sound impressively agricultural. He set off towards the front of the house – and the birds rose from the roof with a clatter of wings as loud as the rattle of tip-up seats in a football stadium when the home team has scored and the crowd leaps to its feet.

'Don't get excited,' Con said to them after a glance round to make sure Maggie was out of earshot. 'We're only just at the beginning.' But of what, he did not know.

The next morning, Arabella peered through the ivy-screened kitchen window and said, 'There's a girl out there. Sitting on the wall.'

Con came and looked, squinting a bit because the sun was so bright compared with the shadowed kitchen. 'It's Maggie Dew,' he said. 'The girl I told you about.' The wall edged a paved yard outside the back door, and Maggie sat there in the sunshine with her bare legs swinging. She wore shorts made from a pair of hacked-off jeans.

'You don't waste any time, do you?' said Neil. 'We haven't been here five minutes and you've got yourself a girl-friend. Good going.'

Con scowled and said, 'It's not like that,' but Neil was unrepentant. 'I admire your taste,' he said. 'She's a cracker.'

'Do they have milk on her farm?' asked Arabella, sniffing suspiciously at an opened carton. 'This smells a bit iffy. Must get this fridge working.'

'It's just that the power points are the old-fashioned sort,' said Neil. 'Round pin.'

'I *know*,' said Arabella. 'Ask her in, Con.'

Con ate the last of his bread and peanut butter and went out, licking his fingers. 'Hi,' he said. 'My mum says come in.'

'No, thanks,' said Maggie.

'But – she wants to know if you've got any milk. I mean, if your farm has cows.'

'We're arable. You can't buy milk from farms anyway, that has to go off in the tanker, get pasteurised. I'll fetch you some from the shop, though.' Maggie jumped down from the wall.

'That would be great,' said Con. 'Hang on, I'll get some money.'

Maggie shook her head. 'You can pay Mrs Fosdyke when you go down there. I'll tell her who it's for. How much d'you want?'

'A litre, I should think. Shall I come, too?'

'No. I'll go on the bike. Won't be long.' She retrieved the bike that was leaning among some weeds and coasted off.

Con felt vaguely miffed. His own bike was somewhere, but in all the confusion of yesterday, he hadn't seen where the men put it. In one of those mildewed old stables, perhaps, that Neil was going to convert into garages and workshops. He went back into the kitchen and poured himself some rather warm orange juice.

'Isn't that sweet of her,' Arabella said when she heard about Maggie and the milk. 'People are so much nicer in the country. I tell you, it's going to be brilliant here, I just know it.'

Neither Neil nor Con answered. Neil raised his eyebrows and dropped a tea-bag very neatly into the cardboard box that was serving as a bin. Con knew what the gesture meant. Things here might not be brilliant at all. The whole thing might be a huge mistake. Who could know?

There is no need to know. Just keep on.

The words were placed in Con's mind as precisely as Neil's dropping of the tea-bag, and he almost gasped.

'The builder's coming at ten,' he heard Neil say. 'Barker.'

'Heavens, yes,' said Arabella. She glanced at her watch and made a face. 'Any minute now. I meant to be up really early, but I didn't get to sleep for hours. I did my deep breathing and everything, but it didn't work. Unusual for me.'

'Nobody could sleep with all that scrabbling and scratching going on,' said Neil. 'Sounds as if the place is running alive with rats. Getting rid of those'll have to be Barker's first job.'

Arabella nodded regretfully. ''Fraid so. Awful, having to kill living creatures, but they just wouldn't mix with teaching Yoga.'

'Oh, I don't know,' said Con, who had recovered a bit. 'Share your mat with a rat.'

Nobody smiled. Arabella was looking positively worried. 'The public health people would have a fit,' she said.

'It could be birds,' Con said without really meaning to.

His parents stared at him. 'But birds go to sleep at night, don't they?' said Arabella.

'Sleep-walking birds,' Neil suggested – but this

time, Con was the one who did not smile.

Sleep-walking birds. The idea fitted exactly into the dream-filled night from which he had not long woken, full of rustling feathers and the gentle grip on his wrist of big, grey-scaled claws.

'Could be owls, of course,' said Neil. 'Or bats. Par for the course if it turns out we've got bats in the belfry.'

But Arabella simply wasn't up to any teasing this morning. 'Give me a break,' she said.

Con finished his orange juice and went out to wait for Maggie. *Bats. Batty. They put her away.* He thought now about the full meaning of what Maggie had said yesterday. The girl who wanted to fly across the sea to freedom had ended instead behind bars. Locked up.

Caged, Conan. She was caged.

With a black flapping of wings that split the sunlight, the great crow came out of the sky to land with quite a heavy thud on the wall where Maggie had sat. The blue eyes stared with sharp intelligence, and Conan took a cautious step forward.

Tell me, he said in silence. *I want to know what happened.*

But Maggie came rattling into the yard on her bike, and the crow opened its wings again and lifted away into the morning sky.

'Mrs Fosdyke says you can drop the money in when you're passing,' said Maggie. She handed Con a litre carton from her saddle-bag, then grinned. 'You won't need much milk, not if you're going to start up this Centre like people say. Just feed them on carrot-juice – I seen a place like that on telly.'

'That's health farms,' said Con. 'Yoga Centres do proper food. At least, we will. Vegetarian, but lots of it.'

'That right?' Maggie was still grinning, and Con mentally kicked himself. The Bardini-Smith ability to take a joke really was a dead duck this morning.

'You coming in?' he asked. Arabella would be waiting for the milk.

Maggie shook her head. She turned away and did up the straps of her saddle-bag.

'Why not?'

'Just because.'

'Because what?' Con demanded.

She wouldn't meet his eye. 'The Hall. We don't none of us go in there.'

'But *why*?'

'Because that's *haunted*,' she said in exasperation. 'I didn't want to tell you. I mean, you got to live in it.'

'Oh, come on!' Con felt quite angry on behalf of his new home. Just because there were a few funny noises going on, and this sense of strangeness – 'You

19

can't blame the house,' he said. Somehow he was sure Wilderness Hall wasn't the cause of whatever was happening. The big rooms that looked out across the fields were innocent, and so were the stairways and the turreted bedrooms and the crazily old-fashioned bathroom with its mahogany fittings and massive brass taps. Even the rustling in the attic did not seem in any way threatening. 'It's a nice place,' he argued. 'It's just that something –' He couldn't put it into words.

'Something,' Maggie agreed. Her grey eyes were meeting his with a new directness from under her thatch of hair. 'But what?'

Con shrugged. He wasn't sure how much he could say to her without the risk of being laughed at. 'There's a sort of – sadness,' he said. 'As if something happened here that can't be forgotten.'

Maggie didn't laugh. She didn't even look away. After a moment's thought, she said, 'Do you reckon a house can remember?'

'I don't know,' said Con. 'I think something remembers. But it might not be the house.'

'What, then?'

He shrugged. Birds . . . dreams . . . This was dangerous territory. He didn't want to sound as if he was off his head.

Maggie was watching him. 'I won't tell anyone,'

20

she said. 'You don't have to worry.'

'It's not that.' But it was, of course. As Neil had said about the Lottery win, *If one person knows, they all know.*

The roar of an approaching car made them both look up. From inside the walled yard, they couldn't see it, but the crackle of heavy tyres over gravel grew louder, and Maggie said, 'Sound like it's coming in here.'

'It'll be the builder,' said Con.

'Not Barker?'

'Yes. Why?'

'You just be careful,' Maggie said.

A large American pick-up truck turned into the yard, glossy black, with a big spotlight on the roof and roll-bars that looked as if they would see off a buffalo.

'Wow,' said Con.

A huge man climbed out of the truck and came towards them. He wore a tweed jacket that looked tightly stretched over his massive shoulders, and a brown felt hat. 'In the kitchen, are they?' he asked.

'Yes, I'll show you,' said Con.

'No need, boy.' The word sounded more like 'bor' in his heavy Suffolk accent. 'I int no stranger to this house.' The man walked past them to the kitchen door.

Maggie looked at Con and said, 'You best get in with the milk. He'll be wanting his cup of coffee.' Then she got on her bike and rode away.

In the kitchen, Mr Barker had sat down at the table, on a bentwood chair which suddenly looked very insubstantial. He had not taken his hat off, just pushed it to the back of his head. His eyes were of no particular colour, greyish brown, like stones.

'Oh, good, you've brought the milk,' Arabella said when Con came in. 'You'll have a cup of coffee, Mr Barker?'

'Woont say no.' The builder joined his bulky fingers comfortably, and Con saw that he wore a very expensive-looking watch on a gold bracelet so stretched by his thick wrist that there were gaps between each link.

Arabella was raking in a cardboard box. 'I was sure we had some biscuits,' she said.

'Don't bother on my account,' said Mr Barker. 'I int no man for biscuits.'

He looked, Con thought like a man for bricks and concrete and tons of cement. Above all, a man for money. *You just be careful*, Maggie had said.

Ignoring Arabella, Barker looked across at Neil and said, 'So you bought the Hall.'

'As you know.' Neil had no patience with people

who stated the obvious, and he sounded crisp.

Barker eyed him for a cold moment, then remarked, 'That's a funny old place, the Hall.'

'Funny?' enquired Arabella.

'Not what you'd call funny har har.' The builder's slow speech made the idea ridiculous. 'There's a lot of folk won't set foot in here.'

'Old places are always like that, aren't they?' said Arabella cheerfully. 'Tales of a grey lady with her head under her arm.'

'All part of the charm,' Neil agreed.

The builder sat back in his chair, causing it to creak dangerously. 'Charm,' he said. 'Well, I int never heard it called charm. Not by nobody.'

'Mr Barker,' said Neil in the precise voice which meant he was getting annoyed, 'if you'd rather not work here because you think the place is haunted, then by all means say so, and we'll find another builder. No point in wasting each other's time.'

Barker stirred his coffee untidily and said, 'You won't find no one better than me, bor.'

'I'm sure you're right,' said Arabella, sounding flustered. 'We looked in Yellow Pages, and your entry was much the biggest, wasn't it, Neil?'

Neil gave her a warning glance and turned back to the builder. 'But if you're not happy with the deal –'

'Int a question of happy,' said Barker. Con

wondered if happiness had been written off, together with biscuits, as too trivial to bother with. 'Fact is,' the builder went on, 'all the small firms get their stuff from me. Breeze blocks, cement, roof trusses – you name it. So you won't do yourself no favours going to them. I can do it cheaper.' He took a sip of coffee and then put the mug down on the table and wiped his mouth on the back of his hand. 'I tell you what, though,' he went on. 'If so happen you find this place int for you – never mind why – just say so. "Mr Barker, we made a mistake, we're putting it back on the market." I'll only charge you for work what's been completed, never mind what's been agreed to. I won't hold you to no contract. Can't say fairer than that, can I?'

'It's really nice of you,' Arabella said. 'But we wouldn't dream of putting the Hall back on the market, would we, Neil? I have this feeling it's been waiting for us all these years. If we can just get rid of the rats.'

'Rats,' said Barker thoughtfully.

Arabella nodded. 'I'm sure it must be rats. In the attic. We were awake half the night.'

The builder gave a single, decisive shake of his head. 'Int no rats in this house, missus. If I been in that attic once, I been a dozen times. No nests, no droppings. No rats.'

'Well, if it's not rats, what is it?' asked Neil. 'There's certainly something.'

'You're right, bor,' Barker agreed. 'There is something. And you want to know what that is?' For the first time since he had come in, he smiled. 'That's the Bird Boy.'

And Con's mind was suddenly full of beating wings.

Three

The three of them stared at the builder. Neil was frowning and Arabella looked worried. 'You mean there really is a ghost?' she asked.

Barker's smile took on an extra satisfaction. 'That depend, don't it,' he said. 'Call it what you want.'

Find out, find out.

The urgent words were sharp in Con's mind. 'The Bird Boy went away, didn't he?' he said. 'He just disappeared.'

'What?' said Arabella, startled. 'How do you know?'

'Maggie told me.'

Barker looked disapproving. 'You don't want to believe all what people say. What they don't know they make up.'

'You're right about that,' agreed Neil.

Arabella was still staring curiously at Con, but she shifted her attention to the builder and said, 'Gossip can be so unkind, can't it. All this talk about

Mr Fothergill's young wife being mad. She was probably just desperately lonely.'

'She were a relative of yours, I hear,' said Barker. So he did his share of listening to gossip, Con thought.

Arabella nodded, a little reluctantly. 'She was my grandmother's sister. Larina. It means Seagull,' she added.

'Does it?' Con was fascinated. 'How amazing. It all fits, doesn't it? Her wanting to fly away across the sea and everything.'

'We can talk about that later,' said Neil, with a touch of disapproval. 'Right now, there are practical things to discuss.'

'I could go and pay for the milk,' Con offered. He'd find nothing out from the builder if they were going to talk about money and cement.

'Great.' Arabella fished in her purse for money. 'Get some bread as well. Brown. And orange juice, and see if there are any fresh vegetables.'

'D'you know where my bike is?' asked Con.

'No idea,' said Neil. 'You'll have to go and look for it. Try the stables.'

Outside, he walked across the walled yard and turned right up the track Barker had driven along in his pick-up truck. It led round the side of the house, joining with the main drive and then curving round and under an arch into the stable yard. Con came to a halt on the sun-warmed flagstones. There was something about this place that he didn't like.

The crow was sitting on the roof.

Look, Conan. You must look.

Oh, all right, Conan thought irritably. *I am looking, aren't I?* No need to nag.

It's more than you think.

Small birds were clustering on the ridge-tiles. *Here's the audience again,* Con thought. *What's the matter with you lot?*

There was no reply.

Con had glanced into these stables yesterday and seen that they were full of old junk and musty hay, but he looked again, in search of his bike. Deserted stables ought to be great for exploring and mucking about in, but these were just sort of dank and rotten. It must have been nice once, Con thought, with harness jingling and the clatter of hooves and trundle of wheels, but the silence now was ominous, and the gaping doors that hung off their hinges contained dark interiors that seemed full of sadness, as if the vanished horses regretted their lost lives.

The crow was sitting above the last stable on Con's left, where there was a bit more floor space than in the others. No bike, though – just an old cart, with its shafts propped up against the wall, and the empty stalls where horses had stood.

Con went on, under the second arch at the far end that had a clock tower built above it, and the birds whirled away towards the trees. The drive ran on between gateless pillars to the open fields, but on his left was a long, creeper-covered wall with a wrought-iron gate in it. Con lugged it open with some difficulty, and found himself in a walled garden. It was hot and still, with butterflies busy among the rampant growth of nettles and poppies and bitter-smelling ragwort. Overgrown trees sprawled along the old brickwork, and wasp-hollowed apples and plums lay on the ground amid a buzzing of wasps. Against the far wall was a gate like the one he had come through and a row of low-built greenhouses with holes here and there in their green-filmed glass.

Working out the geography, Con realised he had come round in a circle. This garden backed on to the track between it and the kitchen yard, which made sense, as they must have grown fruit and vegetables here. Under the weeds, there were still traces of dark-glazed, barley-sugar edging tiles that had marked the beds and paths.

He found his bike in the first greenhouse, leaning against the staging together with Arabella's. He hauled it out from among the clutter of seed trays and old flower pots and the dry, grey coils of what had once been a garden hose. The removal men must have bunged the bikes in the first weatherproof place they came to. Or perhaps they, too, hadn't much liked the stables. No, that was ridiculous. Removal men didn't go around testing the atmosphere, they just got on with the job. Con wheeled his bike on to the track, then mounted it and set off along the stony surface.

Once out on to the road, the going was less bumpy and Con cheered up. This was better than London, with its jam-packed traffic. Fabulous being able to whizz down an empty road instead of having to ride in the gutter because of the cars and vans and buses. You could even make a right turn without risking your life. In their old house, he'd been permanently banned from the main roads, which meant he could only do miserable little runs down the side streets or – big deal – to the park and back.

The village lay on the other side of the level crossing. There was a pub, then some houses and a small post office, and Con had almost ridden past the shop before he spotted it, standing back behind some trees. At first glance, it looked like a flower shop, half-smothered in an array of blossom and greenery. Seed boxes full of small plants were stacked outside the windows, autumn pansies in all sorts of colours but most of them green-leafed things which Con couldn't identify. There were plants in pots, too – geraniums and herbs and biggish shrubs. Gran would approve of that, he thought. There wasn't much she didn't know about plants. He parked his bike under one of the trees and pushed open the door.

A bell tinged above his head as he stepped into the shop. The place smelled of washing powder and dog biscuits and apples, and in spite of the row of self-service shelves, it wasn't at all like a supermarket. Sacks of chicken meal and pony nuts were heaped on pallets standing on the floor, and the wooden counter was cluttered with white-labelled bags of scones and buns and trays of eggs, some of which were a peculiar green colour. Con stared at their waxy texture and wondered if someone had dyed them, and the woman behind the counter looked up from her crossword and said, 'Can I help you?'

She was almost as odd as the eggs. She wore a brown hat not unlike Mr Barker's, except that hers had a couple of long tail-feathers from a pheasant stuck in it. They made her look like a mad bird herself, except that she wore an old-fashioned flower-patterned overall.

'Are you Mrs Fosdyke?' Con asked.

'I am. Who's asking?' She had slightly bulging brown eyes, and a hairy chin.

'My name's Con. Con Bardini-Smith. Maggie Dew got some milk for us this morning.' Not for the first time, Con wished his name didn't sound so posh.

'From up the Hall,' said Mrs Fosdyke.

'Yes.'

'Got settled in, have you?'

'Um – sort of.' In fact, the place was a total shambles, with tea-chests standing all over the place and nothing to eat except sardines and tinned biryani, but Con didn't feel he could go into all that.

'Take a bit of time, getting straight,' said Mrs Fosdyke. 'Sixty-eight pence, the milk.'

'We need some orange juice as well. And bread.'

'Help yourself.' She returned to her crossword.

Con investigated the vegetable rack and found bunches of carrots tied with raffia, green runner beans and lots of different kinds of apples in cardboard boxes that had once held something else. There were sacks of potatoes and plenty of tomatoes and lettuces, but the bananas were more black than yellow, and the oranges looked as if they'd been there for months.

'Home-grown,' said Mrs Fosdyke, watching him.

Well, she wouldn't grow bananas, Con thought. Or oranges. He put some tomatoes into a bag, and some bright red apples, and selected a lettuce. Pausing to collect a sliced Hovis and a carton of orange juice, he carried his armful to the counter.

'Got baskets by the door,' said Mrs Fosdyke.

'Sorry, I didn't see them.' He touched one of the green eggs carefully, and looked at his finger. No colour had come off.

'Duck,' said Mrs Fosdyke. 'Mrs Cook's Khaki Campbells. You want some?'

'Not just now, thank you.' Con wasn't sure what Neil would say about green eggs. Arabella would probably love them.

Totting the prices up on a piece of paper, Mrs Fosdyke indicated the labelled bags with her pen and said, 'Treacle scones for your tea? All home-made.'

'Erm – how much are they?'

'Only sixty-five pence. And you know what you got, not like this bought rubbish.' She waved vaguely at the shop as if she disapproved of it.

'All right,' said Con. 'Thanks.' He handed her the fiver Arabella had given him, and got twopence back. He started to gather up his purchases, wondering whether this woman, too, knew about the Bird Boy.

Watching his slowness, she asked, 'You want a carrier?'

'Yes, please.'

She fished a used bag from under the counter and shook it out.

'Maggie says people think the house is haunted,' Con ventured as he put his things into the bag.

Mrs Fosdyke's mouth tightened. 'I never listen to gossip,' she said. She sat down on her chair behind the counter and picked up her crossword.

Con couldn't quite believe this. Everyone here seemed to know all about everything. He made one more effort. 'It's just – I'd really like to know about the Bird Boy.'

Mrs Fosdyke marked in a clue. Seconds went by while Con lingered in hopes of an answer, then she looked up and said, 'Was there something else?'

'Er – no. Thanks.' He went out into the bright afternoon, and the bell tinged behind him.

For a few days after that, Con was so busy unpacking and helping with the sorting-out that there wasn't much time to think about anything else. It was on Sunday night that he woke sharply, sure that it was morning. But it was moonlight that streamed with such brilliance through the curtainless windows, and somewhere out there, a bird was singing a long, babbling song, full of trills and passion. A nightingale, Con thought – they were the

34

ones who sang to the moon, weren't they? He listened. The house was very quiet. The birds in the attic were not walking in their sleep tonight.

I never sleep, Conan. Not now. But I remember it. I used to wake with my nightshirt twisted round me like the jesses that tie the legs of the captive hawk, hot in the heavy bedclothes while the nightingale sang of freedom. I could never make the sound of human words, Conan. They said I was mad. But neither could I sing as the birds do, only clatter and croak like a crow.

What happened? Con asked with his heart thudding. *Tell me.*

There was no answer, and he lay there with the silence of the house rushing in his ears like a distant river. As he listened, the rush grew louder and more distinct, like the noise of fast-running water, quite close. Con sat up, certain that the sound was real. He got out of bed and padded across to the door, opened it and went out on to the landing. Somewhere above his head, water was running – he was sure of it. Moonlight shone across the floor from the big window above the turn of the stairs.

She flew across the sea. Con could not be sure if this was his own thought or if it came from somewhere else. Surely he was not hearing the sea? *Wake up*, he told himself. *You're probably sleep-walking, like the birds.*

He made his way to the bathroom and felt for the domed brass light-switch on the wall.

The glare from the bulb in its flat metal shade was dazzling, and Con put his hand over his eyes. When he took it away, he squinted suspiciously at the heavy brass taps on the basin and the green-stained bath, but no drips came from any of them. He used the toilet and flushed it, hoping that the gush of real water would settle whatever this plumbing mystery might be. As pipes gurgled and the tank in the attic refilled itself noisily, he switched the light off and went back to his room.

He stood just inside the door and listened. If the noise went on, perhaps he should wake Neil and Arabella – but he'd look such a fool if he'd imagined it. On the other hand, what if something was overflowing up there, seeping across the attic floor, filling up whatever overhead spaces it could find until it started to pour down the stairs and through the moulded ceilings, bringing them crashing down? Maybe the whole house was going to collapse. Con started to sweat at the thought of it.

When the tank was full, the flow cut off with a soft clunk, and there was quiet. The nightingale had stopped singing. Con cocked his head, listening intently. There it was again, more distinct than ever, the rush of moving water, like the sea over stones.

Be sensible, Con said to himself. *It must be outside. Neil said there's a pond here somewhere. If there's a pond, there might be a river. Maybe the wind's changed or something, so I'm hearing it for the first time.*

He moved round the end of his bed, making for the window, and had almost reached it when he snatched his foot back. He had stepped on a patch of floor that was warm – almost hot, as if it lay in sunshine or a central heating pipe ran below it. But moonlight held no warmth, and Wilderness Hall had no central heating system. That was to be one of Mr Barker's jobs, installing a modern boiler and radiators. But he hadn't started yet.

Con crouched down and felt with both hands across the carpetless floorboards. Just one of them had this glowing warmth – the rest were cold. He wondered why he was not more scared. *Perhaps I'm terrified*, he thought, *but I just don't know it. Perhaps I'm actually asleep and I'm not scared because this is just a dream.* He heard the rush of water stop, and the silence seemed real. But was it?

Conan, listen. The voice was as close and intimate as though its owner crouched beside him in the moonlight. *Dreams happen to you, don't they, just as things happen when you are awake. While they are happening, they seem real, but when you wake, you wonder. This is real, Conan. When you wake, remember it. Remember you must find the key.*

Con stood up slowly, and moved forward until he felt the warm board under the soles of his bare feet. He was not afraid. There was no smell of burning, no crackle of hidden flame or whiff of smoke – this was a cool warmth, as pure as moonlight.

Cool warmth? Con almost laughed. This whole thing was crazy. But the laughter left him and he gave a small, sudden shiver. He turned to his bed and crept back into the feathery comfort of the duvet.

You must find the key.

Con puzzled for a few moments over the meaning of the words. There was nothing to be heard now except the familiar scrabbling overhead. He was not alone – the sleep-walkers were moving again. He gave a sigh of trust in the unknown watchers, and slid into the darkness of his dreams.

Four

Con woke late the next morning, to the sound of banging and the squeal and grind of an electric drill. He got up, his mind still full of last night's strangeness, and shuffled his bare feet carefully across the floor by the window. All the boards were as cool and dusty as each other. It had just been a dream, then. He trailed into the bathroom and turned on the tap, watching the water flow into the grey-veined basin. He'd been awake enough last night to wonder if he was dreaming. Surely you couldn't *dream* you were wondering if you were dreaming? Now, that really was ridiculous. You'd end up having no idea what was real and what wasn't.

Con dipped his hands into the water and stared at them, moving his fingers slowly in this strange, clear stuff which he would soon allow to run away through its pipes to wherever it went. Drains, sewers, the sea. *Tell me what I should do*, he said silently.

There was no answer.

Con bent and splashed water over his face and neck with both hands, recklessly scattering drops over the floor. Then he pulled out the brass plug and reached for a towel – and a brief statement spoke clearly in his mind.

I am in the cage.

Con gasped, and gooseflesh bloomed on his damp skin like a frightened bird raising its hackles. *Why?* he asked. *Where? How can I find you?* But his frantic questions were not answered.

When Con went downstairs, the front door was standing open, and workmen were lugging in toolbags and lengths of copper pipe, together with a three-legged contraption to bend them on. Monday morning, and Barker was making a start.

Arabella was sitting in the kitchen with shade-cards spread about on the table. She looked up and said, 'Hi – what colour d'you want your bedroom?'

'Black,' said Con, then shook his head. That was to do with crow-feathers and moonlight.

'Sounds a bit Gothic,' his mother said. 'You're not starting on a phase of skulls and nose-rings, are you?'

'No,' said Con. 'Could be blue,' he amended. 'Like the sky.' Sky-blue eyes. This wasn't getting any better.

40

'M'm.' Arabella selected another shade card and sat back, frowning over it. 'Tricky colour, blue. There's a truly awful pale blue they use on breeze block walls in primary schools. Hits you in the eye like a talcum powder tin.'

'I know,' Con agreed. 'We had it at Albert Road.'

'At least the school here isn't blue,' said Arabella. 'Whoever designed it must have had a thing about fire stations. All those shiny pipes, and the red paint.' Then she remembered. 'Oh, Lord – you start tomorrow, don't you?'

Con nodded gloomily. Not that Marston Middle seemed particularly awful. The headmaster had been quite friendly, smiling a lot as he held up a sample of the school sweat-shirt, red, with a rising sun logo – but there was something a bit weird about the way the place stood in a field among other fields. Very agricultural. Sheep, stubble, sugar-beet, school, stubble, sheep.

'We'll have to go into Bury and get a sweat-shirt,' Arabella said. 'He seems quite fussed about everyone being in uniform.'

'Suppose so.' Con didn't want to go into Bury. He wanted to stay here in Wilderness Hall, in case he was needed. *You must find the key*. It was like being given a job which you didn't understand although you knew it was important. The dead opposite from school, really, where everything was made very clear, but none of it seemed important. From tomorrow, he'd be taken away from the Hall for seven hours every day, and the unknown, important job would be left unattended to. *I am in the cage.* A boy who had once been real – a boy who shared Con's name – needed help, though Con had no idea how to provide it.

'What's the matter?' Arabella asked. 'You look miserable. Is it just school?'

'Mostly,' said Con. He'd told his mother about the Bird Boy, who had disappeared from the Hall that should have been his, but he didn't want to talk about the key he had to look for or about the words which someone or something spoke so clearly in his mind. Not that Arabella wouldn't believe him – quite the opposite. She'd be so impressed and concerned that she'd never give him a moment's peace. And it didn't seem right, somehow, to tell other people about something which was so deeply private. All else apart, there was quite a risk that he'd sound totally insane – and his mother was already upset enough about the rumours that Larina had been not right in the head.

'Take some vitamin C,' Arabella advised. 'And St John's wort, that'll cheer you up. You've probably got autumn sadness, with the days drawing in. And

42

moving house is very stressful. I'll just give the workmen some tea, then we'll go into Bury, right?'

'Right,' said Con.

Just let it happen. The words were conversational – cheerful, even.

It was ridiculous advice, Con thought. How could he do anything else? *Don't get much choice, do I?* he said – and somewhere, on the face of a boy he could not see, he caught the ghost of a smile.

'That's better,' Arabella said, looking over her shoulder at him as she filled the kettle at the tap. 'You're really pretty good at relaxation.'

Mr Barker's American pick-up truck crunched into the yard as the three workmen were sitting round the table. He walked into the kitchen with another man behind him and looked round with disapproval. 'You int paying this lot to drink tea,' he said to Arabella. 'They gets their lunch-break and that's plenty.' Then he indicated the man who had come in with him and added, 'This here's Arthur. My brother. He'll be doing your electrics.'

Arthur made no move to shake hands. He was much skinnier than his brother, and had a silent, ferrety air about him. He wore a brown and orange Fair Isle slipover with a hole in it, and his shirt sleeves were rolled up over scrawny arms.

Arabella smiled at him, but Arthur didn't smile back, just nodded, so she turned to his larger brother and said, 'If he's Arthur, which Barker are you? Just so I know which one to ask for if I happen to phone.'

'George,' said Mr Barker. He took a leather wallet from the breast pocket of his tweed jacket, extracted a card from it and gave it to her. 'You want me, you can get me on the mobile,' he said.

'Thanks,' said Arabella. 'A cup of tea for you both?'

'Coffee,' said Mr Barker. (Con couldn't imagine anyone calling him George.) 'Tea for Arthur, though. If that's all right.'

'Fine,' said Arabella, but with her eyebrows up a little, as if she thought he might have said Please.

The builder looked for an empty chair, and one of the workmen got up quickly to let him sit down. The other men finished their tea hastily and one of them said, 'Best get on. Thanks, missus.' They went out.

Con asked, 'There isn't anything leaking, is there? I mean, something in the house that would make a noise like rushing water?'

'Could be.' Barker put his wallet back in his pocket without hurry.

'What do you mean, Con?' Arabella asked. 'When did you hear this water?'

'In the middle of the night.' He thought about the warm floor board, but decided to keep quiet about that.

'Poltergeist,' said Barker with satisfaction. He almost smiled.

'What's a poltergeist?' Con asked.

'Any geist that polters,' Arabella said cheerfully. 'A ghost that moves things about. Turns taps on, causes fires, makes cold winds blow. That sort of thing.'

Neil came into the kitchen in time to hear this, and groaned. 'Don't start again,' he said.

'Sorry,' said Arabella.

Mr Barker spooned a lot of sugar into his coffee and stirred it. 'If you don't want to know what go on in this house,' he said, 'then I won't say nothing.' He and Arthur exchanged glances. Con almost grinned, because the pair of them were a bit like Laurel and Hardy, those old-fashioned comics – a good double act. Except they weren't really very funny. They were too calculated for that, and too heavy.

'But I *do* want to know,' said Arabella, determinedly cheerful. 'I'm all agog. Whatever happens here is very much our business, so we need to be in the picture.'

Neil sat down at the table, looked exasperated. 'I have to tell you I've no patience with this stuff,' he said, 'but we may as well get it over and done with. What is all this about a poltergeist?'

Arabella drove the big Volvo along the winding lanes in silence, and Con stared out across the dry fields. A scorched whiff came in through the car's open windows from the black stripes of stubble-burning. Mr Barker's tales had been alarming. Hot coals thrown across a room, papers swept from a desk as if by an invisible hand, cups shattering of their own accord. Even Neil had been reduced to a worried silence, though, as he said afterwards, they only had Barker's word for it.

'Maybe we should get the place exorcised,' Arabella said as she changed gear for a particularly sharp corner.

'Exercised?' Was this a different form of Yoga?

'Exorcised. It means saying prayers for the repose of unquiet souls. A kind of religious service.'

'But you don't believe in religion,' said Con.

'I don't believe in the *Church*,' Arabella corrected. 'I think God is in all things, and religion is a way of understanding that, and respecting it. But maybe whatever is so restless in the house is the spirit of someone who believed in the Christian Church. It might need the business of bell, book and candle before it can settle.'

Con shook his head. 'It's not like that,' he said.

'How do you know?' Arabella braked to let a pheasant run across the road, then went on again.

Be careful.

The warning was to Con, not to the driver. 'Just – it doesn't feel right,' he said. Mr Barker's stories had sounded like silly games. Charades, Murder In The Dark. Made-up stuff to give you a scare like a spooky video. Click the switch and it was gone. Nothing to do with the real strangeness of the house and the people who had lived there. Con glanced at his mother's anxious face and wished he could tell her what he was involved in. But he didn't understand it himself yet, and the warning words were clear. This was not for sharing. Not yet.

'I do hope we haven't made an awful mistake, coming here,' said Arabella unhappily. 'It's all right for Neil, he doesn't let any of this stuff get to him, but I can't help wondering if we've done the wrong thing. And I love the place so much, that's the trouble.'

'It isn't wrong,' said Con. 'I'm sure it isn't.'

'Really?'

'Yes, really.'

Con knew he spoke the truth. But as he stared out at the scorched and shaven fields and at the birds wheeling lazily in the afternoon sun, he sensed that a grim laughter lay somewhere in this Suffolk landscape. Whatever lay ahead was not going to be easy.

A gentle grasp of claws seemed to tighten round his wrist in reassurance, and two silent words came to comfort him.

Trust me.

The school outfitter's shop was amazingly old-fashioned, with lots of dark wood and a chipped plaster model of a schoolboy dressed in grey flannel trousers and the braided blazer of some posh private school. And over by the glass-topped counter, Maggie Dew and her mother were also buying a Marston Middle Sweatshirt.

'Hi!' said Maggie, waving, and Con saw her say something to her mother. They both came over.

'So you're the new owners of the Hall,' said Mrs Dew. She had the same straw-coloured hair as Maggie, and wore a denim skirt and sandals – not Con's idea of the floury-handed farmer's wife. 'I'm Jane Dew.'

'Arabella Bardini.' They shook hands. 'Lovely for Con to find a friend so soon,' Arabella went on. 'I do hope you'll drop in as well. Come for a coffee – you'll have to forgive the chaos.'

Maggie had moved off to stare at a rack of hockey sticks, and Con joined her.

'How you getting on with Barker?' she asked.

'I don't much like him,' said Con. 'He keeps going on about the Hall being haunted, as if he really wants to rub it in. Mum's really worried about it. Neil doesn't take any notice, though. He says it doesn't matter whether we like Barker or not, the thing is to get the work done.'

'Who's Neil?' asked Maggie.

'My dad.'

'Right.' She didn't ask anything else. 'We're going to the Cash and Carry,' she said. 'If you're going to run this Yoga place, you could get a card to buy stuff there. That's a lot cheaper.'

Jane Dew seemed to be saying the same thing to Arabella, who was looking interested. 'But we're not up and running yet,' Con heard her say. 'We'll need to be in business before we can get a card, won't we?'

Maggie's mother laughed. 'They won't mind,' she said. 'All good for trade, isn't it? And you'll need cleaning stuff and paint and all that. Bed linen, towels, garden tools – no point in paying retail prices.'

'OK,' said Arabella. 'I'm convinced. You go ahead, and we'll follow your car.'

The Cash and Carry stood in a disused airfield. It was a sprawling, flat-roofed warehouse with cars parked all round it on the cracked and weedy concrete that had been a runway. At the glassed-in desk inside the door, Arabella was filling in a form.

'Number catered for.' She tapped her pen against her teeth, pondering. 'Say a dozen people on the course, three of us plus helpers—'

'Put down thirty-five,' said Jane Dew.

'But—'

'You want to sound professional.' She gave what Con was starting to recognise as a particularly Suffolk smile, amused but with a faint contempt for anyone who didn't know the score.

Arabella filled in the number, 35. 'Con, could you be getting a trolley while I finish this?' she asked. 'Save a bit of time.' She was feeling hassled at being watched, he thought. But he was quite pleased to go in search of transport. The trolleys were whacking great things that looked as if they belonged to railways, but as everything here came in packs of a dozen or more, you'd get nowhere with those little wire supermarket jobs. Maggie had come out for a trolley as well, and they pushed them back into the warehouse. Goods were stacked to the roof in avenues of steel shelving, and a forklift truck purred about, getting things down that were too high to reach. Driving one of those must be a fun job, Con thought.

Maggie caught his envious glance and said, 'My brother drives a forklift, down at Knockholts'. Agricultural supplier.'

'Great.'

'Only for the holidays, though,' Maggie went on. 'He'll be going back to college soon.'

'Right.' Perhaps it was rather childish to enthuse over forklift trucks. He wondered if he'd ever catch up with the things Maggie knew and he didn't.

Arabella came to join them, inspecting her newly-issued card. 'You going to do the pushing?' she asked with a smile.

'No, thanks,' Maggie said promptly. 'Boring.' And although he wouldn't have minded steering the big trolley down all those aisles, Con left it to his mother and went outside with Maggie, who came straight to the point.

'So what did Barker say about the Hall?'

Con poured out the list of scary events, and Maggie nodded, unsurprised. 'Told you,' she said. 'That's haunted.'

She sounded almost smug about it, and Con was suddenly angry. 'Yes, but not the way Barker says it is. This poltergeist business is stupid – it's something bigger than that. Something –' he hesitated, not sure what he could say. 'Something sad.'

Maggie looked at him carefully. 'You really like the Hall, don't you?' she said.

'Yes, I do,' said Con. 'I can't imagine living anywhere else.' And to his surprise, he found that he really meant it.

She nodded slowly. 'See, I never heard half of what Barker's on about,' she said. 'We all reckon the place is haunted, on account of the mad woman and the Bird Boy, but all this about fires and taps – you ask me, he made that up.'

'But why?' asked Con.

Maggie smiled a little pityingly. 'He want the place for himself,' she said. 'He's trying to scare you out of it.'

'For himself?' Con was startled. He thought for a moment, then said, 'He did tell us to let him know if we wanted to put it back on the market.'

'I bet he did,' said Maggie.

Con stared at her, thinking furiously. 'But if Barker wanted the Hall, why didn't he buy it? He's got money, hasn't he?'

'Oh, he got money all right,' Maggie agreed. 'But they had to wait, you see. Because of the Bird Boy what disappeared. The Hall couldn't be sold for fifty years, in case he come back. It was in Mr Edwin's will. But the fifty years was up this spring, so that's when it went on the market.'

'Barker could have bought it straight away,' Con objected.

'He tried,' said Maggie. 'He put in a bid for it, quicker than anyone. He'd knock the place down, see, build an estate of houses. But Withers don't like the Barkers. Old Mr Withers fell out with them years back, I don't know why. Some sort of family thing. So Eric Withers didn't take Barker's bid. He sold it to you instead. We was all glad,' Maggie added, but Con wasn't listening to that bit.

'Wow,' he said. 'Barker must hate our guts.'

Maggie smiled her Suffolk smile. 'I reckon he do,' she said.

Five

When they got home, Con went upstairs and felt the boards in his bedroom. They were cold, all of them. He stared out of the window across the fields. A greyish thicket of willow trees stood just beyond the slope of the hill, suggesting the presence of water. Perhaps that was the pond Neil had talked about, Con thought. Sometime he must go and look at it. But not just now. He felt as if he was waiting for something, but he didn't know what. He watched while Barker's men came out and drove off in a van and a rather dilapidated Vauxhall. Then he went downstairs and selected from an open toolbag a long-handled screwdriver and a jemmy with a forked end. He carried them back to his room and laid them on the floor beside the window. Just in case.

Arabella said rather gloomily that they'd all better go to bed in decent time because of getting up for school the next day.

Con lay awake for what seemed hours. He heard the plumbing quieten after Neil then Arabella had been to the bathroom. After a while their murmured conversation in the room next to his ceased, and the light clicked off. But Con was waiting, he could not sleep, must not. His limbs twitched with tension as he lay there, listening to the silence. Tonight, it was broken by the usual scrabbling above him, and he began to feel desperate. It had not been like this last night, when he had woken from the depths of sleep.

Sleep . . . his body began to slacken. All sound had died away, and the quietness was gently humming in his ears. *Humming!* Con gasped, forcing himself awake again. The hum was turning to a rush. He was out of bed before he knew it, crouching to slide his palms across the floor – he snatched his hands back. There it was, glowing with a warmth like the body-heat of something alive.

Hardly daring to breathe, Con reached for the long screwdriver. He felt with his fingers for the crack between the warm board and its neighbours, then pushed the screwdriver hard into it and levered. The board lifted a little way. Con levered again, further along, then picked up the jemmy with its broader, double-pronged blade. The plank came up with a screech of protesting nails, and he glanced over his shoulder in the dark room, half expecting the door to open and an irate parent to demand what on earth he thought he was doing.

Nobody came. Con lifted the board clear. His heart was thumping as he stared into the black, oblong hole it had left. He wished he had a torch – the idea of putting his hand down there to grope for whatever he might find was very scary. As if in answer to his need, the moon sailed clear of the clouds, and its cool light beamed down through the window, showing him that something lay on the joist below the floor's surface. Looking more closely, he could just make out that it was a small key.

Take it.

The instruction made Con jump, even though – or perhaps because – he'd been hoping for advice of some kind. He looked up at the window in case the crow should be staring in at him, black in the paler darkness, but there was nothing. Just the full moon, calm and perfectly circular.

Slowly, Con reached down into the hole. Just before his fingers touched the key, he stopped, afraid it would burn him or unleash a lethal electric current.

No words came, but the room seemed full of smiling encouragement.

The key was not hot, just pleasantly warm. Very carefully, Con picked it up. He got to his feet and stood by the moonlit window, staring at the small thing he held. It was not more than the length of his own thumb, delicately made of blackened brass. He turned it in his fingers, looking at the serrated edges that would engage with some lock, the ridged shank, the handle that was shaped like a cloverleaf with a small hole through each of its round sections. What would it open?

No words. A rush of anxiety replaced the smile, as if this act of trust in a boy called Conan was a big risk.

It's all right, Con said silently. *I won't let you down.*

The anxiety slackened. A bank of cloud drifted across the moon, bringing darkness, and Con shivered. Suddenly, he felt very tired. He crept back into bed and pushed the key under his pillow. He was asleep before his fingers had relinquished it.

In the morning, Con trod the board back into place above the perfectly ordinary, cool joist. The nails, bent by his jemmying, wouldn't go back, and stuck up at all angles. He'd have to borrow a pair of pincers and take them out, he thought. Not now, though. Arabella was shouting up the stairs about breakfast.

He took the key from under his pillow and looked at it uncertainly. He couldn't be sure what lay ahead at Marston Middle – it might be safer not to have anything on him that could be stolen or cause trouble. He bent to put the key back, then couldn't. He wanted it with him. He pushed it deep into the pocket of his new, respectable school trousers and felt the solid, gentle warmth of it there, a small comfort in whatever the day might bring.

'Con-*an*!' Arabella only used his full name as a mark of urgency. 'Come *on*!'

'Coming,' he said.

At the bottom of the stairs, he put the tools back into their bag, then went on into the kitchen and to whatever awaited him in the next seven hours.

Not unusually, they were a bit late getting to school. Nobody had found out where the school bus stopped or what time it left, and Arabella always underestimated the time it took her to drive anywhere. Con wouldn't let her come in with him. It would be the complete kiss of death to be seen being escorted by your mother, if this school was at all like Albert Road.

Con spent some time sitting outside the secretary's office until someone could be found to deal with him, and then Miss Ainsworth turned up, curly-haired and a bit breathless, to explain that she was his Guidance Teacher. She took him up to the form room and said this was a new boy, Con, and a few people nodded – but the real trouble started during the first period, which was English, taught by a man in a spotted bow tie called Mr Dowson.

'Ah,' he said, looking at Con with his bushy eyebrows raised, 'a newcomer.' He consulted his bits of paper. 'From the great metropolis, I understand. Conan Bardini-Smith.'

Someone made the usual sick noise Con had come to expect at the sound of his posh name, but Mr Dowson ignored it. 'Conan as in Doyle,' he went on. 'Author of Sherlock Holmes, as I'm sure you all know.' He turned to Con and added, 'You may find our ways a little slow for you, Mr Doyle, but I'm sure you can show these potato-heads a thing or two.'

The silence was unnerving. At Albert Road, everyone would have laughed and shouted a bit of cheerful abuse, but here, the only response was a narrow-eyed exchange of glances.

'The usual animated reaction, I see,' said Mr Dowson. 'All right, boy, sit down.'

'Get you later,' someone muttered as Con made his way to the table he'd been allocated. Things were not looking good.

Maggie passed him in the outward rush at break-time, and gave him a cheerful smile. 'All right, are you?' Then she was gone, part of a chattering group of girls.

The potato-heads were waiting.

'Here he come,' said one of them.

'So he do,' agreed another, a large, solid boy with bristling ginger hair. 'Going to show us a thing or two.'

Con joined the group. There was no choice.

'Go on, then,' said the first boy. 'What you got that's so special?'

'Money,' said the ginger one. 'His old man won the Lottery, didn't he?'

Miss Ainsworth walked past with a whistle round her neck and a cup of tea in her hand, and smiled at them. The boys smiled back. When she had gone, they turned to Con again.

'How much?'

'When did you win it?'

'What you goin' to do with it?'

'Bought the Hall, haven't they,' said the ginger boy. 'My dad's doing it up for 'em.' He grinned at Con. 'He say your ma's a nutter.'

A rush of fury made Con feel reckless. 'So you're Peter Barker,' he said. 'I heard about you.' *Watch out for him*, Maggie had said at the Cash and Carry yesterday. *He's the youngest one of the Barker lot, and the nastiest.*

'Everyone know us Barkers,' said Pete. He stuck his thumbs in his belt, still grinning. 'And I know about you. Connie Bikini-Smith.'

The others laughed, and Pete suddenly pushed Con in the chest, very hard. Con staggered back, and someone pushed him from behind to make him step forward again. In the next moment, they were all at it, shoving him from every side. Con tightened his muscles and planted his feet firmly, determined to stand his ground, and the pushes turned into thumps. He kept his fists at his sides, knowing that he mustn't lose his temper. If this turned into a fight, he'd get thrashed, one against so many. He hunched his shoulders and ducked his head, pushing his hands into his pockets. And the fingers of his right hand met with the key.

For a fatal instant, Con's thoughts flew to the strangeness of last night, and he was momentarily off guard. A smack in the ribs took his breath away, then someone kicked him on the shin. Con gasped and bent forward, and Pete Barker hit him hard on the left eye.

'Come on, then, townie,' Pete said exultantly, 'show us a thing or two.'

Con's control broke. Hardly able to see through the blinding pain in his eye, he lashed out and felt the jarring thud as his fist caught Pete in the ribs.

'You bugger,' said Pete. He caught Con's wrist and twisted it behind his back as the thumps and kicks went on.

Con was close to panic. *I can't handle this*, he thought. *Help.*

As if in answer, the sky was suddenly dark with the flapping of broad wings. In a rattle of strong feathers and a reek of carrion bird-sweat, the crow was on them, and out of its ragged blackness, scaly talons raked across Pete Barker's scalp like harrow-blades. Then it soared away into the autumn sun, rising above the school roof to disappear into the dazzling sky.

Pete clamped his hands across his head. His knees were bent, and for a moment, everyone seemed paralysed – then Pete slowly released his hands and stood upright, inspecting his palms. To Con's slight disappointment, there was no blood on them.

'Jeez,' said Pete. 'Did you see that?'

The others nodded, open-mouthed.

Con found himself laughing in sudden, wild happiness. *That'll show them!* he thought.

'What you laughing at?' one of the boys asked – but the fight was over, and they knew it.

Pete ran cautious fingers through his short-cropped hair and scowled up at the sky. 'I'll shoot that blasted bird,' he said. 'See if I don't.'

Miss Ainsworth came back from dealing with a cut knee and glanced at the group suspiciously, noticing Con's flushed face. 'Are you all right, Conan?' she asked.

'Fine,' said Con. And the weird happiness made it quite easy to give her a bright smile.

He went home on the school bus, getting off when Maggie did, at the top of the drive that led to the Hall.

'So you got trouble with Pete Barker,' she said.

'Yes.' Con's eye was throbbing, and he felt bruised all over. 'Which way do you go to the farm?' he asked, not sure if she was going to walk down the track with him.

'Along the road.' But she didn't move away. 'What was this about a bird?' she asked. 'People were saying it come down and went for Pete.'

'Something like that.' Con wasn't sure how much he should say about it.

Maggie's grey eyes did not shift from his. 'Something like what?' she asked.

Con shrugged uneasily. And then –

Tell her.

The instruction was quiet, though so clear that Con thought Maggie must have heard it, but her gaze was unbroken.

'All right,' he said. It was a relief to give in. Standing there in the golden light of the September afternoon, he told Maggie about his meeting with the crow on that first day, about the seagull girl who wanted to fly to freedom but never found it, and about the words that came unbidden to his mind as though someone spoke close beside him.

She listened, frowning, and did not interrupt.

'That fit, don't it,' she said at the end with her Suffolk disregard for ordinary grammar. 'If it's the Bird Boy what haunt the place, then he haunt you as well. And they used to call him Crow, my gran said. D'you reckon the crow is kind of him, too?'

'I don't know,' said Con. 'Yes, perhaps. But –' He prickled with the significance of it as he gave Maggie another scrap of dream or memory. 'His real name was Conan. Same as mine.'

Maggie looked at him with disbelief. 'You're making it up,' she said.

Con felt his face flush a little. Could he be sure he hadn't made it up? Not really. 'I might have dreamed it,' he admitted. 'But it seems real.'

'If that's right,' said Maggie, thinking hard, 'it could mean you and him are part of the same thing. Like two halves, only he's dead and you're alive. Maybe he's kind of living through you.' She made a face. 'Creepy.'

Con shut his eyes, scared by the idea. Perhaps people who'd been told they had cancer felt like this, he thought – invaded by something they'd never imagined possible. The Bird Boy wasn't cancer, but all the same – 'I'd rather have myself to myself,' he said.

'That depend if you like him,' said Maggie. 'I wouldn't mind if it was someone nice, like my cat, Minkie. I'd share with her all right.'

'But a cat's real, and a ghost isn't,' Con objected. 'At least, not in the same way.'

'I think ghosts are real,' said Maggie. 'That's why they scare me. But if it's just your Bird Boy at the Hall, and his crow, that int so bad.'

Con was suddenly aware of the key in his pocket, glowing warm as if to remind him of its presence. 'There's this, too,' he said. 'Look.'

The quiet sky seemed to shine with approval as Maggie took the little key and turned it carefully in her fingers while Con explained about its finding.

'That int a door key,' she said. 'Too small. More like for a desk or a wardrobe. That's old, though. Blacksmith made.' She looked up at him. 'What do you reckon it open?'

'I don't know,' said Con. 'There was no furniture in the Hall when we came.'

There was a pause, then Maggie asked, 'Do your mum and dad know?'

Con shook his head.

'You ought to tell them,' said Maggie. 'It don't seem right, you doing all this on your own.'

It was hard to explain. Arabella was already upset and worried, and she so much wanted Wilderness Hall to be peaceful and lovely. Con felt vaguely protective of his mother, because she never seemed to know that things might hurt her. When they'd been burgled by two young house-painters in London, she'd been devastated. 'They seemed such *nice* boys,' she'd wept. 'Why should they have done that? What went wrong?' To Maggie, Con said, 'My mum gets upset. And Neil wouldn't want to know. He doesn't like that sort of thing.'

'Everyone get upset sometimes,' said Maggie. 'And I reckon that's right. If there's bad things happening, you got to get upset about them, else you'd never try to make them better.'

Con felt helpless. 'I don't know where to start,' he said. 'It's so hard to understand.'

'I understand about Barker,' said Maggie practically. 'You got to hang on tight at the Hall, else he'll have you out of there, one way or another. See this field?' She swept an arm round to indicate the ploughed land bordering the drive. 'We'll lose that if Barker get the Hall. He's drawn the plans up already. Told my dad the farm would be smaller, because he want a lot of it for development. There'll be houses here, and the drive will be a road. Street lamps and everything.'

'But he can't do that!' said Con. 'It's not his farm.'

'It would be if he bought the Hall,' Maggie said. 'Like I told you, the farm is part of the estate. My dad rents it from the owner of the Hall. That used to be Mr Edwin years ago, then it was Withers, for the Fothergill estate. Now it's your parents. One day it might be you. Only my dad wants to buy the freehold, so it most probably won't be.'

Things turned a slow somersault in Con's mind. *One day it might be me*, he thought. Owning all this, running the place, making decisions. Until now, it had been purely Neil and Arabella's affair. He, Con, just went where they went, and enjoyed what there was to enjoy. He had never imagined that he might have a stake in it, too. With a new sense of responsibility, he said, 'We've *got* to get things right.'

With a thud, the crow landed on the top rail of the gate beside him and shuffled its wings into place.

'Is that it?' whispered Maggie. 'I mean – *him*?'

'Yes,' said Conan. He caught a flash of blue-eyed interest as the bird turned its head to tidy a tail-feather, and the words which spoke themselves in his mind were surprisingly casual.

Don't worry about the gun. Pete won't shoot me.

Touched on a lurking worry, Con made a small sound of surprise and relief.

'What is it?' asked Maggie.

'Pete said he'd shoot him,' Con said, still staring at the crow. 'But – I kind of think he won't.' In spite of what he had told her, he still felt a little shy of revealing the words he'd just heard.

'Not unless that's daft enough to turn up at the Gun Club,' said Maggie. 'You can only shoot on your own land or else somewhere that's licensed for it.'

Con was not quite reassured. 'But – Pete does have a gun?'

'Oh, yes,' Maggie said. 'Everyone got guns. You only have to own a bit of land, you can have a shot-gun. Keep the vermin down. Rats, rabbits. Crows.' She eyed the black bird uneasily. 'People say they take the pheasant chicks, see.'

'Does Barker have land?'

'Only the yard at Walsham. But he belong to the Gun Club, all his family do. Real expensive guns, he got, all engraved. I seen them. I go clay-shooting with Dad sometimes.'

Con stared at her, impressed. '*You* shoot?'

'Just a four-ten,' said Maggie. 'I don't like twelve-bores, they're too heavy. Make your shoulder sore.

You must come some time, have a go.'

'Great,' said Con. But in spite of the crow's promise and Maggie's breezy confidence, he felt shadowed by dread. *He's living through you*, Maggie had said. In this open place, there seemed no safety, and no hiding place from this awful responsibility.

'I best be getting home,' said Maggie. She looked at him and added, 'You all right?'

'Fine,' said Con, as he had done to Miss Ainsworth.

Maggie went on regarding him for another second or two, then she said, 'See you tomorrow, then.' And walked away down the road.

Con set off down the rutted drive to the Hall. In the hedge beside him, a black shape seemed to flit through the pattern of leaves, keeping him company, though whether it was the crow or just his imagining of it, he could not be sure.

Six

When Con went in through the back door, Arabella was leaning against the kitchen sink, sipping a mug of camomile tea – he could smell the thin bitterness of it from where he stood. Bad news, he thought. His mother always turned to camomile tea when she was upset – she said it was calming. But right now, Arabella did not look calm. Her hair was escaping from a wildly grubby chiffon scarf tied round her head, and there was a black smudge on her cheek. 'Hi,' she said, managing to smile. 'How did school go?'

'All right,' said Con. 'What about you?'

Arabella closed her eyes and shook her head. 'Don't ask,' she said. 'We've had a fire.'

'No!' Con's mind flew at once to the warm board in his room. 'Where?'

'In the bathroom,' Arabella said to his relief. 'Mr Barker was working up there – he's doing the plumbing himself, to make sure it's a really good job, he says. So sweet of him. It's just as well he was up there. The wires that led to that old heater had shorted, he said, somewhere under the bath. And the pipes had been lagged with rags, and they were smouldering.'

A likely story, Con thought.

'He burned his hand,' Arabella went on, 'and the bathroom was full of smoke; we had to flap towels and things to get rid of it. The men said it was the poltergeist, of course. Neil was furious, but I don't know.' She stared into her mug unhappily. 'I can't help wondering what will happen next.'

'Did he burn his hand badly?' Con asked, narrow-eyed. Unless there were decent-sized blisters, he wasn't going to be convinced.

'I don't know,' said Arabella. 'He was terribly good. Bundled the rags into a bucket even though they'd burst into flames by then, carried it all downstairs. There are smoke marks all over the wallpaper.'

'But what about his hand?' Con persisted.

'Well, by the time he came back, he'd put a dressing on it. He's got First Aid stuff in the pick-up truck. A plaster and lots of acriflavine – that bright yellow stuff. You can't buy it any more, it got banned for humans, but he gets it from the vet. He says it works wonders.'

'Huh,' said Con.

His mother stared at him. 'What's got into you?' she asked. 'One day at school, and you come back all cynical. I was really scared, Con, can't you see? Neil had gone down to the village, I was all alone – I don't know what I'd have done without Mr Barker.'

We've got to get things right, Con thought. 'The thing is,' he said, 'Mr Barker could have started it himself. He's *trying* to scare you. He wants us out of here so he can get the place for himself.'

'That's *ridiculous*,' Arabella said. 'What are you thinking of, Con? You can't go round blackening someone's name just because you don't like them very much.'

'It's not that. Maggie said –' And Con poured out the whole story.

Arabella lost her temper. 'So you think that's news, do you? Let me tell you, Con, Mr Barker was perfectly honest with us about the whole thing. He admitted he'd have liked to buy the site, but he's looking at somewhere quite different now, the other side of Bury.'

'So he says.'

For a moment, Con and his mother stared at each other, both of them angry. Then Arabella put her fingers to her forehead and murmured, 'Calm.' She was wearing an old shirt of Neil's over a faded Indian skirt. For a moment she said nothing more, then she slowly dropped her hands and looked at Con afresh. 'Heavens,' she said. 'What have you done to your eye?'

'Bit of an argument.' Con was starting to feel shaky. The day had been a bad one, and a row with his mother was the last thing he wanted.

'You mean a *fight*? Con, that's awful. Why? Who was it?'

'There were quite a lot.' He could hardly mention Pete Barker at this moment – it would sound as if he was just scoring a point.

Arabella started fishing about in a still-unpacked box on the floor. 'There should be some arnica in here. And Rescue Remedy – yes, here we are. Take a few drops, I expect you're still in shock.' She handed Con the small dropper bottle. Neil always said the stuff was just straight brandy, Con reflected, but he didn't mind. It tasted quite nice.

'Do the teachers know there was a fight?' his mother asked.

'Miss Ainsworth had to go in with a kid who'd cut his knee.'

'Well, they ought to know.' Arabella found the arnica and tipped some on to a tissue. 'Here, put this on your eye. And sit down, Con, for goodness' sake. Now, tell me all about it.'

Con, holding the cool pad against his eye, gave a slight shrug. 'They were just – saying things about us.'

'What things?'

Your ma's a nutter. No he couldn't tell her that. And he couldn't say anything about the crow, either, not yet.

Not yet.

The unbidden words were clear and firm in his mind, agreeing.

'Come on,' said Arabella.

'It was just – they thought I sounded posh.'

His mother's shoulders drooped. 'Isn't that awful,' she said. 'They've been brought up with all the wrong values, you see. Never learned that there's good in everyone, no matter what they sound like or how they behave. But that's what worries me about your dislike of Mr Barker, Con – do you see?'

'Yes,' said Con. He saw only too well.

When the men had gone home, Con sneaked a pair of round-nosed pincers and took the nails out of the loose floorboard in his room. One of these days, he thought, he'd nail it down – but not yet. Not while the sound of banging would cause awkward questions. He stood by the window with the bent and twisted nails in his hand, staring out across the

74

tranquil fields and feeling heavy with responsibility.
I wish I was free of all this, he thought.

You will be. But not yet.

The words filled Con with panicky anger. What had started out as a fascinating puzzle was turning into a kind of imprisonment. Wherever he went and whatever he did, some unknown presence watched him, waiting to use him for its own purpose.

I'm not up to all this, he said silently. *I can't handle it. I'm sorry about what happened to you, but it's over. Leave me alone.* His eye was throbbing and he felt shaky all over. *I'm really sorry*, he said again.

There was no answer.

Minutes went by. The golden light of afternoon shone across the fields, and the house was quiet. A new fear crept in to replace Con's anger and desperation. His words had been accepted. The small spirit of the Bird Boy, who had tried to live through him as Maggie had suggested, had given up and turned away. Now Con would never know what might have happened. He had blown his chance to help the boy who shared his name, and for the rest of his life, he would regret it. There would be no freedom, because the oppressive sense of duty had been replaced with guilt, and that was worse.

I'm such an idiot, he said.

A sharp pain in his hand made him look down.

Without meaning to, he had clenched his fists, forgetting about the twisted, rusty nails he held. A couple of their points had gone quite deeply into his skin. Holding his breath with the discomfort of it, he removed them carefully, then sat down on his bed in an ache of misery. Everything had gone wrong.

Conan. The voice was gentle. *Don't be upset.*

Con gasped, making a sound that was somewhere between a laugh and a sob.

I need you, Conan. Please.

Yes, said Con.

With the simple word, peace came. He waited, but the silence went on and on. The trials of the day began to slacken their hold, and he gave a small sigh and lay down. Within a few minutes, he was asleep.

His hands were sore because they were grasping iron bars at a window, staring out at the sky. *That's where I belong. I should be part of it.*

Flying. Oh, glorious. Wings lean on the strength of the air, spread feathers feel the balance like fingers. Down there, very small, is the house where a woman stares out, her hands gripping the bars.

Sail down in a long curve through the air, land on the window sill, tuck the wings into place, shuffle the feathers so they lie in comfort. *I will always be a crow*.

The woman holds her hand out to a boy and opens her fingers. The palm is red-marked, and on it lies a small silver seagull on a delicate chain. *Wear it next to your heart*.

Now it has changed. A different house, darker, with cedar trees outside, and men walk about in black robes like wingless crows. There are boys everywhere. Pain. *One – two – three* – an arm goes up and down under the whiteness of the ornate ceiling, and the leather belt cuts through the air.

A seagull flies, white and beautiful.

A boy is sobbing beside a stove where mutton boils, his head in the aproned lap of the kitchen woman. Her rough hand strokes his hair. *There*, she says. *There, there*.

Over the curve of the hill, a man drives a black horse along a track. A big man, sitting on the box of a blue-painted cart. His whip traces a fine pencil line through the air. Another man sits beside him, and they are laughing. In the blue, autumn sky above them, crows wheel, and the harsh sound of their cawing mingles with the men's laughter.

'*Caaa! Caaa!*'

The crow's harsh voice cut through Con's dream,

and his eyes flew open. The big bird was standing on the window sill, staring in.

Con sat up. He could feel the neatness of the folded wings as if they were part of his own body, the feathers lying in comfort.

Caged.

Fuddled with dream, the word could have been of his own making.

'Who is caged?' he asked aloud – but the crow took off, riding the air in a strong curve that took it away to the distant elm trees. Con swung his legs to the floor and went to the window, to gaze out after the bird.

His fingers registered a roughness in the frame where his hand rested, and Con looked to see what it was. He saw a group of four screw-holes that had been painted over but not properly filled. In sudden suspicion, Con glanced across at the frame on the other side. There was a matching group of holes, and other groups all the way up on both sides, a hand-span apart. The hair crawled on the back of Con's neck. This window had been barred. For somebody, the room had been a cage.

A choking sense of imprisonment sent Con bolting across the floor and out of the door. He ran down to the hall and to the great front door and heaved it open. He hadn't been this way since the removal day, but he didn't want to go through the kitchen and get stuck with Arabella all over again. Out in the sun, he ran down the mossy steps to the drive, then paused as his heartbeats slowed. It was better out here. After a moment, he turned left and followed the drive round the house and under the archway into the stable yard.

An exhausted silence hung over the place as though no more could be said, at least for a while – but the birds were clustered on the roofs and a lot of them flew above Con as he walked across the flagstoned yard with its cobbled drainage channel running down the middle. He tried to ignore them, wanting only to clear away the clinging cobwebs of his dream, and went on towards the clock-tower arch that framed a view of parkland and fields. As he came into the shadow it cast, a clamour of protest rose from the birds, and he paused, glancing through the open door of the end stable where the old cart was. The place had been swept and tidied. Sacks of cement stood on pallets, and sawn timber was stacked by the wall, together with plumbing fitments and a pile of sand on a polythene sheet. Barker was storing his stuff there. *So what?* Con thought. The birds were making a fuss about nothing.

He went on through the arch and followed the

drive between big trees and thickets of overgrown shrubs until he came to the stone gateposts with their rusted, empty hinges. After that, the drive joined a rough cart-track that led across the fields. The late afternoon was quiet, and no wind moved the trees or disturbed the fleshy green of the growing sugar-beet. Con gave a sigh of relief. It was great to feel ordinary, out here for no purpose except to look around him and breath the warm air.

The sugar-beet gave way to a stubble field, and the grove of willows lay a little way ahead. That's where the pond would be, Con thought. But before he reached it, he came to rough grass that sloped down to a sprawling mass of brambles. Even from where he stood on the track, Con could see the glossy blackberries among their prickly trail of stems, and the rich smell of them drifted to his nose.

The next half hour went peacefully by as Con worked his way from one cluster of ripe fruit to the next, picking and eating. The berries were perfect, full of autumn sweetness, and when he thought of them packed into squishy little punnets in the supermarket, it seemed amazing that hundreds of pounds' worth of fruit simply hung here, free for the taking. His fingers purple with juice, he moved slowly through the prickly tangle that clutched at the legs of his school trousers, but came at last to a place where the ground under the bushes fell steeply away to a greenish gleam of water below him. This must be the pond.

Too full of blackberries to bother about picking any more, Con retreated to the grass where the willow trees he had seen from his room leaned down to the water. After this dry summer, the pond was half dried up, a long way below the surface of the track that ran beside it, and covered with a growth of green weed. And, Con saw, people had been using it as a dump. An old fridge lay under the brambles, and the half-submerged window of a washing machine looked up at him from the scummy greenness like a reproachful eye. The ancient remains of a van stuck up from the water, too, and a rusted bed-spring hung from where it had caught on a branch. He was glad he had done his bramble-picking before he found this. *Why do people spoil things?* he wondered.

The sun was level with the hedges now, and Con turned to go back to the Hall, suddenly despondent. Beyond the trees in the other direction, he could see the roofs and barns of the farm where Maggie lived. Perhaps he'd go over there and see her one day. But not now.

The crow wheeled above him. '*Caaa! Caaa!*' Its raucous cry was very real. Or maybe this was a different crow – there must be dozens of them.

Whatever it was, it circled again above his head, calling in its harsh voice, and as Con tried to continue on his way, it flapped close across his face, wing-feathers almost brushing his cheek. He ducked involuntarily – and the crow flew across the grass to his left, then landed and called again. '*Caaa! Caaa!*'

'Oh, all *right*,' said Con. 'What is it?' He walked across the rabbit-nibbled turf to where the big bird stood and watched him, and when he was almost close enough to touch it, the crow gave a flying hop that took it across a flat slab of stone, to land on the other side.

Conan, look.

A flat slab of stone. Perfectly level, and at one end, a smaller stone with a curved top, lying sideways in the long grass. This was a grave. Con knelt by the fallen headstone and parted the long, wind-dried grass with his hands, expecting to find a name cut into the stone – but there was nothing. Patches of orange lichen made the only patterning on the unmarked surface. Whoever lay here had lost not only life, but all identity.

The crow rose into the evening sky, and Con was alone except for somebody long-dead who lay in the ground below him. He got to his feet and took a few steps backward, still staring at the blank stone. Then he ran.

Seven

'It's Larina,' Arabella said. 'I just know it is.' She let her fork fall to her plate and stared at Con as he came to the end of his story.

'Rubbish,' said Neil. 'More likely a dog or something.'

'It's too big,' Con told him. 'It's – well – human-sized.'

'A horse, then. If there was a grave on this property, Withers would have mentioned it.'

'Perhaps he didn't know,' said Arabella.

'Of course he knew. People round here know everything.'

'But I mean – my friend Isabel says she's going to be buried in her garden. She bought a cardboard coffin and painted it with roses. She keeps it under her bed.'

'That'll be a big help to her relatives when it comes to selling the house, won't it,' said Neil. 'Bones turning up in the potato patch.'

'Perhaps that's why Withers didn't tell you,' Con remarked. 'He might have been afraid you wouldn't buy the place.'

Neil nodded. 'That's a sensible suggestion,' he said. 'Or it may not be a grave at all.' He sprinkled some more Parmesan cheese over his tagliatelle.

'But he told you she committed suicide,' Arabella pointed out, 'so they wouldn't have been able to bury her in the churchyard, would they? Suicide was supposed to be a mortal sin. You couldn't lie in consecrated ground if you'd taken your own life. That's the Church for you. Full of rules.'

'You can't have religion without rules,' said Neil. 'That's what it's about. It's a system.'

Con only half-listened as his parents wrangled over this point. He couldn't see that it mattered much where you were buried. Nicer, in fact, to be out there on the grassy hill than packed into some churchyard with hundreds of others. He ached all over, and the arguing voices began to drift into a dream.

Arabella reached across the table and put her hand over his, giving it a little shake. 'Go to bed, love,' she said. 'You've had quite a day.'

And Con went.

When he came down to the kitchen in the morning,

Neil was sitting at the table as if he'd never left it, reading a letter. He glanced up and said, 'Cornflakes?'

Con helped himself. 'Where's Arabella?'

'Still asleep. We were late last night – sat up, talking. And things have been getting her down a bit. She could do with a lie-in.'

'Yes.' Con knew exactly how she felt. He very much wished he was still in bed himself.

'Your gran's coming to see us,' Neil said, tucking the letter back into its envelope. 'Be up on Friday.'

'I hope she likes it,' Con said with one eye on the clock. Seven minutes until the school bus. 'After all, it's her money.'

'She thinks it's great. We brought her up here to see it in June, remember? Before we bought it.'

Con went on shoving in the cornflakes. He was glad Aussie Gran was coming. She'd cheer things up – she was always good for a laugh.

'Quite a shiner you've got there,' Neil remarked. Con's black eye was a rich plum colour this morning, in spite of the arnica. 'How's it feeling?'

'Not too bad.'

After a slight pause, Neil said, 'Who did it, Con?'

'Pete Barker.' The truth was out before Con thought about it. But things seemed easier today, somehow. 'I didn't tell Mum,' he added. 'She thinks Mr Barker's OK.'

'He probably is, as a builder,' said Neil. 'And that's all I'm interested in. No reason why his son should go around beating people up, though,' he added. 'Shall I have a word with the school about it?'

'Please don't,' said Con. Getting known as a tell-tale wouldn't help. 'It's about us winning the Lottery, you see. They think we're posh.' The sort who complain.

'For God's sake,' said Neil. 'Why do people get in such a twist about money? We haven't turned into monsters just because my mum had a lucky gamble.'

Con stood up and grabbed his school-bag. 'Got to go,' he said.

'OK. Hope you survive all right.'

Maggie, waiting at the end of the drive, almost echoed Neil's words. 'All right, are you.' It wasn't a question, just a Suffolk greeting.

'Such a lot's happened,' said Con. And he told her all about finding the grave, and about the dream he'd had during his brief sleep in the afternoon.

As he came to the end, Maggie gave a little shiver, hugging herself as if she was chilly, although the morning sun was already warm. 'Good thing I met you before all this business started,' she said. 'I might think you'd made it all up else. Except for the woman shut up in the bedroom. That were the Bird Boy's mother. The loony.'

Con felt a rush of indignation. 'You shouldn't say that,' he objected. 'It's easy to think people are mad, just because you don't understand them.'

'The birds understood her,' said Maggie. 'My gran don't remember her, being only a baby at the time, but *her* ma said the woman used to walk about with a cloud of birds all round her. But it got so she wouldn't come indoors, and they was putting food out for her like a wild thing. She'd have died in the winter.'

'But she did die,' Con said. For a moment, his mind was back in the dream, knowing the sensation of how the air ran through your wing-feathers. Was it madness to understand too much? He pushed the thought away. 'I wonder if it was true about the school,' he said. 'It must have been a school, mustn't it? The place where he was beaten, and the masters wore black gowns.'

'Don't know,' said Maggie. 'We could find out about the kitchen woman, though. If that were the Hall, they'd have had someone from the village. Gran and Grandad will know about that.'

'She might even be alive!' Con was suddenly excited. 'Wouldn't that be great!'

Maggie shook her head. 'It's more'n fifty year ago all this happened,' she said. 'So it int likely.'

'No,' Con admitted in a chill of disappointment.

'She might have family, though,' Maggie went on. 'I'll ask.'

'Have your grandparents always lived here?'

'Oh, yes. Not my dad, though – he come from Woolpit.'

Con laughed. 'Woolpit's only a few miles away,' he said. 'I've seen the signpost.'

'I don't see that's funny,' said Maggie.

'It's just that my family come from all over,' Con explained. 'Mum's Italian, though she was born in London, and Neil comes from Australia. He doesn't sound very Aussie, because he's been here since he was fourteen. My gran does, though,' he added. 'She's coming to see us this weekend.'

'And you got an Italian gran as well?'

'Not now. She died when I was quite small.'

'Pity,' said Maggie. 'She might know what happen to the Bird Boy. Maybe he went to Italy.'

Con frowned. 'I don't think so,' he said. 'Mum still writes to her aunt in Verona. She'd probably have known if he'd gone there.'

The bus pulled up, and its doors hissed open.

'See you,' said Maggie, and went to sit with some girls who were waving from the back. Con slid into an empty seat and stared through the window at this place which he had to leave all day. The crow, perched on the gate, stared back.

The potato-heads were waiting.

'Here 'e come,' said Pete.

The others shifted their chewing-gum and grinned. They were standing in a casual-seeming group that blocked the doorway. Fine, Con thought. The bell hadn't gone yet, there was no need to be near the door. But they bawled after him as he turned aside.

'Oy, Bikini, where you going?'

'Come here!'

'Come an' talk to us!'

Pete's half-broken voice cut through the others. 'Bought anything nice, have you? Sports car? Helicopter?'

It was no good, Con would have to join them. Already, heads were turning to see what the yelling was about. Reluctantly, he went over.

'Oh, what a lovely black eye,' said Pete. 'Fell over, did you?' And, still grinning, he trod with his booted foot on the toe of Con's trainer, pressing hard and slowly shifting his weight forward.

'*Don't!*' Con hadn't meant to cry out, but the pain of his crushed toes was excruciating.

The rattle of black wings made him gasp. How

could the crow be here, when it had been sitting on the gate as the bus left? Could it fly that fast? He caught the glimpse of a blue eye, then the crow settled on his shoulder, big claws taking a firm grasp through his sweat-shirt. The hard-feathered bulk of it rustled close against his ear, and the greasy smell of it filled his nostrils.

Pete stepped back. 'Bloody 'ell,' he said.

One of his henchmen waved an arm at the crow and said, 'Gerroff! Shoo!' The bird did not move, but settled its weight more firmly on Con's shoulder.

'Go on, bugger off,' shouted Pete. 'Bloody thing.' And he swung an open-handed slap at the bird, as if to knock it off its perch.

Wings flashed out in warning. '*Caaa! Caaa!*' The raucous cry was shockingly loud, the big beak wide-stretched in anger – and the same anger flowed through the grip on Con's shoulder to charge him with sudden, furious electricity. His fists were clenched and his heart pounded in a blaze of rage. 'All right,' he said to Pete. 'Come on, then, if you want to fight. I don't care if you kill me.'

'Don't be stupid,' someone muttered. Uneasily, one or two of them backed away.

Pete's grin had faded. Without warning, he lashed out at Con – but the crow was faster. The jab of the curving grey beak had happened before anyone had properly seen it, and Pete's elbow was up to protect his face – but they all saw the small, round hole on the back of his other hand, just above the clenched knuckles. A bruised, blue circle surrounded it, and it was welling with blood.

Pete stared at his hand, then at Con, and took a step back. 'You're mad, you are,' he said. He backed a little further and added, 'You're another one like that crazy Bird Boy. You oughter be locked up.'

A crowd had collected, full of excitement about the big bird on Con's shoulder.

'Isn't he sweet!' said a red-haired girl. 'Can I stroke him?'

'If you want your eyes pecked out,' said one of Pete's gang. 'He's a killer.' He sounded rather admiring.

The girl reached out a cautious finger, and the crow did not touch her, just raised its neck feathers a little. 'Our hens do that if you disturb 'em,' said the girl, then added to the crow, 'Aren't you nice! Don't be scared.' She stroked one of the grey claws that gripped Con's shoulder.

'That int scared of nothing,' said Pete, sucking his injured hand. 'Kev's right, them crows is killers. It was one of them killed my dad's grandfather.'

Listen, Conan, listen! The voice was excited.

'What do you mean?' Con asked. 'How did it kill him?'

'I int telling you,' said Pete, sulkily. And the bell went.

The crow's wings brushed hard against Con's cheek as the big bird pushed off from his shoulder and rose into the morning sky. The lifting of its weight left him feeling light and strangely happy, as if he, too, need not be bound to the earth unless he chose.

It's going to be all right, he thought. *I know it is.*

At break-time, Pete and his friends kept away from Con, though there were a few shouts of 'Loony!' and 'Bird Boy! Lock him up!'

They were easy to ignore. The red-haired girl came up with some of her friends and asked, 'Where's your crow? Has he gone home?'

'Don't know,' said Con. 'He can do what he wants.'

'How did you get him so tame?' The others piled in with questions as well.

'Did you bring him from London?'

'How old is he?'

'Are you the boy from Wilderness Hall?'

He could answer that one. 'Yes. My name's Con.'

'I'm Jan,' said the red-haired girl. 'And this is Gemma and that's Kate. How did you find your crow?'

Be careful.

The warning was sharp in the air, and Con frowned. He knew he mustn't spread the mystery around, but he had to tell this girl something. 'You'd better ask the crow,' he said with a stroke of inspiration. 'It's nothing to do with me.'

He saw Maggie out of the corner of his eye, hanging around just close enough to hear what was going on. Then a van stopped outside the school in a blast of jangling *Greensleeves*, and she said, 'I'm going to get some crisps. Anyone coming?' They went off with her like a flock of chattering sparrows, and Con sent his silent thanks.

The school day dragged on, but at last it came to an end, and Con found himself walking down the drive to the Hall. *How did you kill Mr Barker's grandfather?* he asked the cloudless autumn sky that might hold the ghost of a boy – but there was no answer. Con wished he could have talked to Maggie about it, but she had stayed on at school for Gym Club. He knew what she'd have said, though. *Barker's the one what know. Why don't you ask him?*

She was right, of course. The only trouble was, Con didn't want to ask Barker anything.

Walking in through the back door, he found the builder sitting at the kitchen table, going through suppliers' catalogues. It was what Arabella would have called Meant, Con thought.

He took a deep breath and said, 'Mr Barker, can I ask you something? I was talking to Pete, and—'

'My Pete, is that?'

'Yes, and he said—'

Barker was grinning. 'I heard you had a few words,' he said. 'You want to keep on the right side of young Pete, boy.'

'I know.' The black eye made it very plain that Con had not kept on the right side of him, but he pressed on. 'Pete said your grandad had been killed by a crow. And I wondered —'

The builder had stopped smiling. He surveyed Con carefully as the half-formed question hung in the air, then said, 'I weren't going to tell you about that, boy. Woont want to scare you.'

Not much, Con thought. He made himself meet the stone-coloured gaze, and waited.

'My grandad started up as a builder and general handyman,' Barker said. 'And he were the one what took care of things at the Hall. Mr Fothergill's right-hand man.'

'Edwin Fothergill?' The Bird Boy's father.

'Not so much Edwin, no. He were a sickly man, died not long after he came home from his travels. That wife of his were too much for him. It were his younger brother looked after the place after that.

94

Sebastian. Mr Seb, folks called him. A proper gent, by all accounts, but he weren't practical. And a place like this, bor, with the farm and all, take a lot of managing. As your dad will find out.'

'So your grandfather ran it for him.' Con was not going to be side-tracked.

'Like I'm tellin' you,' Barker agreed. 'Now, Mr Seb were plagued by his brother's boy what were left when his ma done away with herself. Connors or some such name.'

'Conan. Same as me.' *I mustn't sound excited*, Con thought.

'That right? Any road, this boy were mad, like his ma. Run about the place a-flappin' and squawkin', skinny as a broom pole, weighed no more nor a bunch of feathers. Mr Seb did what he could for him – sent the lad off to a school what cost a lot of money, but it didn't go no good. He came back mad as ever. Then he disappeared.'

Con nodded. 'I know. But what happened to him?'

'That's what we'd all like to know,' said Barker heavily. 'But the thing is, bor, on that very same day when the boy went, my grandad and Mr Seb was coming up from the farm in my grandad's cart, him driving. Now, there's a pond by the track up there, used to be a quarry.'

'Yes, I've seen it,' said Con.

'Then you'll know there's a good lot of brambles grow down there,' Barker went on. 'And Annie Marsden what worked at the Hall had took her basket to gather some. She were a good cook, they say, made a lot of jams and jellies and that. Any road, she saw what happened. This crow come diving down at the horse's head, she say, screechin' like a thing demented. Now, Captain were as steady a horse as you could wish, but a thing like that, it took him by surprise. He reared up, lost his balance. Fell sideways and took the cart with him, the whole lot went down the bank into the water, and that's deeper'n it look.' He surveyed Con's aghast face and went on, 'The broken shaft went clean through my grandad's chest, killed him stone dead. And as to Mr Seb – it were five hours afore they found him. Had to drag the pond.'

Con stared at him, struggling with the dream that was sharp in his mind again. The cart, the black horse – and then it dissolved into a worse vision as a drowned face came up through the green, weedy surface, water streaming from its dead mouth. And the poor horse – 'What happened to the horse?' He didn't want to hear, but he had to know.

'Horse were all right,' said Barker. 'If the shaft hadn't broke, the weight of the cart would have dragged him down, but he kept his nose above the

96

water and they got him out. I weren't born when it happened, but I remember Captain. My dad had him a long time.'

'What colour was he?' asked Con – but he knew the answer.

'Black,' said Barker. 'Jet black all over.' He clipped his pen into his pocket and folded the catalogues.

A new thought had struck Con. Perhaps it wasn't Larina who lay in the grave up there. 'I found a kind of slab near the pond,' he said. 'I thought it might be a gravestone. Is it where your grandfather–'

'That it int,' said Barker with indignation. 'My grandad were buried in the churchyard, decent and proper, along of Mr Seb. That place you're talking of is where they put the mad woman.'

So we were right, Con thought, and a small shiver ran over his skin.

The builder was sitting back in his chair, one meaty hand resting on the table as he surveyed Con. 'Old Withers didn't tell your ma and pa about her, did he?' he said.

Con shook his head, then wished he'd said he didn't know.

Barker laughed, showing broken brown teeth. 'He wouldn't, would he. Didn't want to scare off a cash buyer.'

Urgency filled Con's mind, but he tried to sound

casual as he asked, 'What happened to her? People say she committed suicide.'

'That she did,' said Barker with satisfaction. 'In the self-same pond, boy. If my dad told me once, he told me a thousand times. A Saturday, it was. Mr Seb and my grandad had been out with the hunt. They was coming back to the Hall, pink coats and all, and Annie Marsden come running out in a terrible state. The mad woman had got away. Weren't Annie's fault, she couldn't hold her, not without help, fighting and scratching like a wild cat, she were, run off across the fields in her bare feet and her night-clothes. So my grandad and Mr Seb turned their horses and went after her. She beat them to it, though. When they got to the pond, there she were, floating like a water-lily. Dead.'

They hunted her, Conan. To her death.

Con felt his face drain of blood, as though he himself had plunged under the surface of deep water. He stared at the builder in horror.

Barker got up from the table. 'So this place bin a bit funny ever since,' he said. 'Like I told you.' He went to the door and opened it, then looked back. 'You know what I'd do, boy?'

'What?' asked Con, dry-mouthed.

'I'd tell your ma and pa they best get out of here, before anything happen.' The stony eyes stared into

Con's, and he was suddenly more afraid than he had ever been in his life. This man was threatening him.

'What kind of thing?' he managed to ask.

'Could be a nasty accident,' said Barker. 'Maybe to them, maybe to you. Never can tell.' Then he went out, and the sunshine that had lit the room through the open door was cut off as he closed it behind him.

Eight

Maggie was sitting on the steps that led to the terrace when Con went out the next morning. She came across to join him, looking excited. 'You'll never guess what I found out!' she said. 'My gran and grandad remember the woman that worked here. Annie Marsden, she was called.'

'That's right,' Con agreed. 'Mr Barker told me.'

'Oh.' Maggie looked faintly miffed. 'You know all about it, then.'

'Quite a lot.' As they walked up the lane, Con went through Barker's story of the crow and the accident, and the poor, mad girl who had run across the fields to her death. When he came to Barker's hint that something nasty might happen to Con or his family, Maggie nodded.

'He's trying to scare you off, right enough,' she said. Then she added, 'Did he tell you about Mrs Fosdyke?'

'The woman who works in the shop? No – what about her?'

Maggie grinned triumphantly. 'That's what I was going to say. She's Annie Marsden's daughter. Flo Marsden, as was.'

'No!' Con stopped in his tracks, staring at her. 'So she knows everything!'

'She know what her ma told her,' Maggie corrected in her slow, Suffolk way. 'And that might not be much. Flo weren't born until after Annie left the Hall.'

Con felt a bit ashamed of rushing on with his own story instead of listening to Maggie. 'What happened, then?' he asked.

'Well, Barker's grandfather and Mr Seb was killed like you say,' she went on. 'So there weren't no job for Annie, with the Hall empty. They was all gone, see. First Edwin, then his wife, then the Bird Boy disappeared and Mr Seb and old Barker died, so Annie went back to her parents in the village. Next thing, everyone can see she's going to have a baby. And Annie says it's Mr Seb's, and they was engaged to be married. Would have been, if he hadn't got himself killed. She was reckoning on being his wife and living in the Hall the rest of her life, the grand lady.'

Con nodded slowly. It all made sense now. 'If she

knew something about Sebastian and Barker's grandad,' he said, '– something they'd done that was bad – then Seb would want to shut her up. Maybe that's why he was going to marry her. Make her part of it.'

'Part of what?' asked Maggie. 'I don't see what you're on about.'

'It's going to sound stupid,' Con said, 'but I can't believe the two men died by accident. There's something too neat about it – the way they drowned in that same pond where Larina died, and on the very day the Bird Boy disappeared. It's as if they were being punished.'

'But what for?' Maggie was frowning. 'You think they hunted the woman like she was a fox or something, but you can't be sure. Could have been like Barker say, she ran and ran, and they never caught up with her.'

'Perhaps.' But Con's mind was running on something else. 'The Bird Boy disappeared that day. But who's to say he went *after* the men died? Could have been before. Could have been they knew, and that's why they were laughing. With him out of the way, the Hall was theirs. I think they killed him.'

A twittering of small birds burst from the hedges, then fell silent.

'You can't prove it,' said Maggie.

'I know.' What's more, Con thought, it was a dangerous thing to say. What if Pete Barker got to hear? 'Best forget it,' he added. 'I could be quite wrong.'

'I won't say anything,' Maggie promised. She always seemed to know what he was thinking.

'So what happened to Flo Fosdyke?' Con asked.

'She had a bad time of it,' said Maggie. 'Annie went to the lawyers, Grandad said, trying to prove she was going to be Mr Seb's wife, but she never got nothing. Went on living with her parents, no one ever married her. It was a big disgrace then, having a baby if you weren't married, so little Flo didn't have friends much. Never got invited to parties or went out to tea. People thought she weren't respectable.'

'That's awful!' said Con. 'I mean, my parents aren't actually *married* – they don't believe in it. That's why I'm Bardini-Smith. I've got both surnames. But we're a proper family.'

'Sure,' said Maggie. They were both silent as they walked, thinking of the child who had no friends. *You don't want to listen to gossip*, Mrs Fosdyke had said to Con. She had learned the hard way to ignore it, all through those years when she was a little girl in cotton frocks. Difficult to imagine it, the way she was now, a cranky woman with pheasant feathers in her hat.

'We've got to talk to her,' Con said. 'We've absolutely got to.'

'You'll be lucky,' said Maggie. 'Flo Fosdyke don't talk to nobody, not about that sort of thing.'

And then they saw the bus pull up at the end of the lane, and had to run for it.

'Here come the loony!' Pete Barker yelled as Con and Maggie came in from the bus park. 'Caaa! Caaa!' He flapped imaginary wings while his henchmen fell about laughing.

'Take no notice,' Maggie said to Con.

They heard her.

'Got a girl to hold your hand?'

'Yah, nannie's boy!'

'Maggie Dew your girl-friend, then?' There were wolf-whistles and yells.

Red-haired Jan came up, ignoring the boys, and said, 'Where's your crow?'

'Don't know,' said Con. Pete picked up a pebble and shied it at him, and he ducked.

'There he is,' said Maggie, pointing.

The crow was sitting on the school roof, just above the doorway. The boys saw it, too. 'Right, you're going to get it,' said Pete. He hauled a heavy catapult out of his pocket and fitted a stone to its thick rubber, then let fly.

The girls gasped, and Con, too, felt a moment's terror. The shot had gone straight for the bird – but the crow rose gently into the air for a moment then resettled, folding its wings as if undisturbed.

'You don't want to do that,' Maggie called across to Pete.

'Oh, no? You just watch me.' Pete fished in his pocket for another stone – and the crow came off the roof like a black flash, diving towards them. Pete dropped the catapult and Maggie, to Con's astonishment, dived to snatch it up then hurl it high over the hedge.

There were cheers both from the girls and some of the boys, most of whom had nothing to do with Pete and his gang. Then Jan shouted, 'Look!'

The crow was flying above them with the catapult dangling from the grip of its claws. It landed in its original place on the roof, and everyone laughed and clapped as they saw the powerful beak tearing at the rubber, the black-feathered head jerking to and fro.

'Hey,' breathed Jan, 'that's creepy.' None of Pete's henchmen said anything. They, too, were watching the crow, open-mouthed.

'You just wait,' Pete said. 'That int goin' to be so clever with a twelve-bore, I tell you.'

Maggie laughed. 'You can't kill that bird, Pete

Barker,' she said. 'Not with a shot-gun nor anything else. That int going to die until it chooses.' And she walked off, the other girls with her.

'Stupid cow!' Pete shouted.

Con turned away as well, walking across to the fence that edged the car-park. He hoisted himself on to the top rail and perched there, waiting to see if Pete's gang would come after him. But none of them did.

Arabella was talking distractedly to Neil as she rolled out pastry on the kitchen table. 'So weird,' she was saying, 'the way it kept colliding with the window.'

Con dumped his school bag. 'What did?'

'This bird. A hen chaffinch – you always know which is which, because the males have pink chests. The females are just brown, with a white flash on the wing. She kept hitting the glass. I was unpacking books in the big sitting room, and I heard her thump against it. But again and again. I mean, why?'

'Saw her own reflection, I expect,' said Neil. 'Birds are pretty stupid things.'

'I wondered if it was that,' Arabella agreed. 'I went out and stuck some parcel tape on the glass, but as soon as I came in she started again. One of the male birds kept diving at her, trying to chase her away. You could see he thought it was peculiar.'

'Well, at least *he* had his head screwed on,' said Neil.

Arabella looked at him broodingly. 'It gave me the shivers,' she said. 'Each time she hit the glass, she almost knocked herself out. She'd fall and flutter, then recover a bit and do it again, as if there was something that I couldn't see, but she could. It was utterly creepy.'

Neil sighed. 'You're determined to find a ghost, aren't you?' he said. 'But any house that's stood for a couple of hundred years will have seen accidents and deaths – it's perfectly normal.' Arabella took a breath, but he held up his hand. 'No, hang on a minute, I'd like to get this straight, once and for all. I agree with you that when people are scared or unhappy, the emotion they feel might set up some kind of resonance in the building. We know that stone and timber and slate are made of subatomic particles, same as we are, so these might get printed, so to speak, with the feeling they've absorbed. But–'

'That's exactly what I'm saying!' Arabella interrupted. 'The human spirit can live on in a place that's been charged up like you say.'

'No.' Neil put his hand flat on the table as if to hold down all silly ideas. 'You're going too far. It may be that we get a feeling of being connected with things that have happened before, but you do have to remember that they're not happening now. Once people have died, that's it. The end. We're the ones living now. We're in charge. Whatever they felt and did, it's finished. They've gone.'

'But what if they can't go?' Con asked. 'If something's gone wrong and they're stuck? In a sort of cage?'

'Sheer imagination,' said Neil. 'That's exactly the kind of thing I mean. Once you start believing your own nightmares, you've lost all grip on reason. It's dangerous stuff.'

'I suppose you're right,' said Arabella. Then she added, 'While you're sitting there, could you grate some cheese for me?'

'Sure.' Neil went across to the fridge and got out a lump of Cheddar.

'What happened to the chaffinch?' asked Con.

Arabella looked guilty. 'I didn't notice,' she admitted. 'I was so busy with the books. I suppose she must have gone away.'

Con nodded. After a few moments, he went outside and walked up the flight of shallow steps that led from the kitchen yard to the terrace. He knew what he was going to find.

The chaffinch lay below the window from which Con had first seen the crow. Her eyes were closed.

He picked up the neatly-feathered body, and the head fell limply sideways. *Why?* he asked in an ache of sadness. *There was no need to do that. You could still be alive.*

A flock of small birds flew out from the grey branches of the wisteria that grew against the wall of the house, and Con turned to watch them wheel away westward, over the roofs of the stable and the clock-tower.

As if replacing them, the crow landed on the stone balustrade with a soft, heavy thump, and turned its head to look at Con out of one blue eye, then out of the other. For a moment, Con wondered if he was just believing his own nightmares, as Neil had said. This crow was living now, and the Bird Boy must be dead. Ghosts were always dead, weren't they? So there couldn't be any connection. Or at least, that's what Neil would say.

Con wasn't so sure. The boy who bore his own name was left behind, in a time that had gone, but who was to say time couldn't make its own connections? It might be like air, a thing that was impossible to see or touch, and yet which was in everyone and everything. Air surrounded the feathered body of the little bird Con held, and it might equally surround and carry its spirit, to become part of all air, or maybe to live again –

nobody could tell. But you couldn't separate one bit of air from another bit – it was all part of one thing. Time could be the same. Just because you could only live in your particular bit of it, there was no need to assume that your time wasn't a part of all time.

It was such a big idea that Con knew he was only nibbling at the edges of it, but he hung on to the small shred he could understand. Someone whose own time had ended could still be around, trying to do something. But having no body of his own in which to live and move, he had to use someone else, whose time was now.

Yes.

Agreement washed into Con's mind with easy simplicity – but the comfort of it did not last long. *So I am being used,* he said, and stared again at the little bird in his hands. His new understanding had come only because she died. Perhaps she, too, had been used. *Do I have to die?* he asked in sudden terror.

For a few electric moments, there was no reply, and when words did form themselves in his mind, they evaded the answer to his desperate question.

It will be all right. And the crow unfurled its wings and took off into the endless sky.

He'd better go and look for a spade, Con thought.

At least he could bury the little bird – it was better than driving himself bats over something he couldn't properly understand. He walked back along the terrace, down the steps and across the kitchen yard. There were tools in the stable where Barker was storing his stuff, he seemed to remember.

The birds flew ahead of him as he went under the arch into the stable yard. They settled thickly on the roof above the door he was heading for, and their twittering stopped as he pulled up the kick-bolt on the lower half of the door. Yes, he was right about the tools. Behind Barker's pallets and timber, a cobwebbed pitchfork stood against the flaking whitewashed wall, with a couple of wooden hayrakes. There was a dung-fork as well, and a shovel and a rusted sickle. And a spade. Con moved towards it – and as he did so, the small key in his pocket made itself felt in a sudden glow of warmth.

Con stopped, puzzled. He'd carried the key with him ever since he found it, and hadn't thought about it much in the last day or two. But now what? Was there something here he should notice? He stared round, looking for anything which the key could possibly unlock – but the wooden-sided stalls where the horses had stood were empty, and so were the iron hayracks, and there was nothing to be locked or unlocked in the mildewed harness that hung from wooden pegs on the walls. The rotting piles of straw had been swept out, and the place was clean, though shadowed and dusty. He went across to the cart that stood with its shafts up against the wall, and looked into it, staring under the wooden driving seat and into the open back with its slatted sides. The tail-board hung down, rusted chains dangling. It was easy to see that the cart contained nothing – and yet Con kept looking at the wooden wheels and the flaking remnants of its blue paint. Was this the cart pulled by the black horse, Captain, who had just managed to keep his nose above the water?

The shaft had broken, Barker said. *Went clean through my grandad's chest.* This cart had two complete shafts. But when Con went closer, still holding the dead bird carefully, he caught his breath. Peering closely at the shafts in the dim light, he saw that the one on the left-hand side was glossy with varnish, unlike the dull, rough surface of the one on the right. It had been replaced.

Con stared at it for a few more moments, then took the spade and went out. The birds lifted in a flutter of wings as he walked under the clock-tower, and followed him down the drive that ran between the stone posts to the fields. They gathered in the branches of a beech tree that spread golden branches above Con's head, and he looked up at them. 'Here?' he asked aloud.

Their quietness seemed to be an assent. The crow was not with them, Con saw. This was the business of the small birds – sparrows and chaffinches, bluetits, robins, little wrens and a good few he could not name. He laid the dead chaffinch on the grass very gently, and began to dig. When the grave was deep enough, he set the spade aside and knelt down with the little bird in his hands. He wondered if he should say something. Neil hadn't let him go with Arabella to the funeral of Italian Gran. 'All that mumbo-jumbo,' he'd said. 'Much too confusing for a six-year-old.' But a bit of mumbo-jumbo might have come in handy right now.

He looked down at the small, feathered body he held. 'You were a good bird,' he said. 'You did your best.' Somehow, he didn't want the earth to dirty the neat, soft feathers, so he scooped dry leaves into the grave and laid the chaffinch in the clean, brown bed, then covered her with some more. Then he filled in the earth and stood back. *You won't be alone*, he said silently. *I'll think about you.* And perhaps, in her way, she would think about him. He felt strangely comforted.

Nine

A restless wind got up in the night, buffeting round the house and whistling down the chimneys. It mingled with the scuttering of whatever it was in the attic and blew through Con's half-waking dreams, and in the morning he felt chilled and wretched. The sun had gone, and piles of ragged cloud were driving hard across the Suffolk sky.

'You look a bit down,' said Maggie when they met at the bus stop.

'A bit.' Con couldn't face telling her about the chaffinch. He was too tired, and anyway, she'd think it was silly, all that fuss over a bird, when there were thousands of them about.

Maggie fished in her school-bag and got out a Kit Kat. She broke it in half and gave him his share.

'Thanks,' he said.

'When I get miserable, I take the goat out,' she told him. 'That always cheer me up.'

'The *goat*?'

'It was a kid someone gave us. A billy. He was meant for the deep-freeze, but Mum and me got fond of him. So we had him neutered and kept him. We call him William. He's a good lawn-mower. And he likes going for walks along the hedges. Goats like leaves better than grass.' She looked at him and added, 'You got no pets, have you?'

'No. We had a cat in London, twice. But both times it got run over.' He didn't want to think about that.

'Ours has got kittens,' said Maggie. 'You could have one of them, couldn't you? It wouldn't get run over at the Hall, there's no traffic.'

'I'll ask,' said Con. Warm fur under his hand, a long stroke that went all the way to a tail-tip. Yes, he'd like a cat very much.

'Come and see them if you like – you never been up to ours.'

'That would be great. Tomorrow?' Tomorrow was Saturday. No school for two whole days. Wonderful.

'Me and Dad's going clay-shooting if it's fine. I hate it when it's raining. Come on Sunday.'

'OK.' Just as well not to make it tomorrow, Con thought. Aussie Gran would be here – she was coming this afternoon. He began to feel a lot better.

'Hi, Con!' said Gran. 'How're you doing?' She got

up from the table to give him a hug. She wore an orange fleece jacket and a pair of skin-tight cycling shorts, and Con saw to his surprise that she was smaller than him now, though she felt as skinny and tough as ever. 'Looks like you been having a bad time,' she said, grinning at the sight of his fading black eye. 'And the carry-on about this place as well. Never mind. You're winning.' She gave him another kiss, and ruffled his hair. Gran was like that – nothing you could do about it. 'Want a coffee? And what about this ghost? Sounds a cracker.'

'It's been upsetting the staff,' said Neil, straight-faced.

'In other words, me,' said Arabella. 'And there's not much hope of getting any other staff, as far as I can see. The locals won't set foot in the place. Allan Dew was saying people are very superstitious here.'

'He's the farmer, isn't he? Good land over there. I can see why he wants to buy the place. I biked over and had a look.'

'Did you borrow Arabella's?' Con asked.

'No,' Gran scoffed. 'That old bone-shaker? I bunged mine on the train. At my age, I like decent gears.'

'Off her head,' said Neil. 'Went down to meet her at the station and there she was, lugging this bike out. Said I shouldn't have come, she'd have cycled up. Fifteen miles.'

Gran gave Con a wink and said, 'We'll go exploring, you and me, on the bikes.'

That would give the village something to gossip about, Con thought, the mad biking granny from Australia. He grinned. 'You're on,' he said.

That evening was the best one they'd had since they'd been in the house. Gran said she was going to have a flat-warming – not that she'd come to live in it permanently yet, but just to make a mark on it. 'Stir up the old ghosts a bit,' she said. 'Let them know what they've got to deal with.' So there was a lot of trekking up and down stairs to the empty rooms on the top floor that were going to be hers, Neil and Con and Gran carrying chairs and a table and an electric fire and bottles of Australian wine contributed by Gran, while Arabella cooked up something oriental and wonderful in the kitchen. Then Neil went off to Bury in the car because Allan Dew had said there was a late-opening deli, and came back with olives and interesting cheeses and a chocolate gateau and several sorts of exotic ice cream.

Con took his CD player up and sorted out some suitable music – Arabella's favourite Stravinsky and

Neil's trad jazz, Rolling Stones for Gran and a few Golden Oldies of his own, like the Waterboys and some thumping pop just to stir everyone up. The place still looked a bit bare, so he and Gran lugged a sofa up as well, taking an end each – she insisted on being the one who went backwards – and some floor cushions and a couple of Indian throws and a lamp with a pink shade. It left the rest of the house looking pretty bare, but at least it was cosy.

This was the way the Hall should be, Con thought as he sprawled with a leg dangling over the arm of the sofa, comfortably full of chocolate cake and mango ice cream. It had waited years for people to come with warmth and laughter and good food and music, and now it was all happening. The blustery wind that hunted round the outside of the house just made it all seem more warm and secure.

Careful.

The sharp warning puzzled him. He swung his foot to the floor and frowned. The gentle music of *The Firebird* moved into eeriness, with a haunting tune that seemed like the darkness before dawn, just a single orange streak in the sky.

In the next instant, Con jumped half out of his skin. A shattering crash sounded downstairs, then another. Neil leapt to his feet, and all of them pelted down the stairs. 'Damn,' said Neil. 'Half the lights are off – Arthur's rewiring.' He opened the door to the big room where Con had first seen the crow.

Shards of glass lay on the floor in the moonlight, gleaming like a shoal of fish among the broken, distorted pieces of window frame. Cold air blew in through the gaping holes in the tall windows, and another piece of glass fell with a tinkling crash even as Con watched.

'Phone the police,' Neil said, as he skirted round the glass and pushed open the unbroken French windows. He disappeared on to the terrace.

'Where the phone?' Arabella said frantically. They were still using the mobile while they waited for BT to put up poles and wires.

'In the kitchen,' said Con.

Gran was searching about among the glass and debris. 'Must be a brick,' she said. 'Or something. Got a torch?'

'I'll get one.'

He turned as Gran added, 'Nothing ghostly about this lot. If you ask me, someone chucked something. Got to be here somewhere.'

'Yes,' said Con. *Thank heavens she's here*, he thought. Gran was like Maggie, full of common sense. He could feel glass splinters crunching under his trainers as he went out of the door and along the dark corridor that led to the kitchen.

'Wilderness Hall,' Arabella was saying into the phone. 'No, nobody's hurt, but there's a lot of damage.'

Con grabbed the torch from where it stood on the dresser and ran back. His gran was standing with her fists on her hips, staring round. 'Not a sign,' she said. 'That's really odd. Shine the torch round, Con.'

The beam winked back from the shards of glass as it travelled across the floor, but Gran was right. There was nothing that anyone could have thrown.

Neil came in through the French windows and said, 'Nothing out there as far as I can see. No sound of a car or anything.' He looked wind-blown and chilly.

'Well, it must have been something,' Gran said firmly. 'Windows don't break on their own.'

Arabella came in from the kitchen in time to hear this, and gave Gran a dark look. 'You can't be sure,' she said.

'Sweetheart, *please* don't start the creepy stuff again,' said Neil. 'Right now, I really don't think I can stand it. Mum's perfectly right, there's got to be some cause. Are the police coming?'

'They're on their way,' said Arabella. And even as she spoke, they heard the crunch of tyres coming fast up the drive, and the sky outside began to pulse with a flashing blue light.

'Pretty good,' Neil said. 'Must have had a patrol car in the area. They're going round the front.'

Everyone went through the hall to the front door. A policeman was already coming up the steps, shining a powerful flashlight. 'Mr Smith?'

'That's me,' said Neil. 'Do come in. I'm glad you've got a torch – we're in mid-renovation and there's no electricity in the room where this happened.'

The police torches cut through the darkness like sword blades, lighting up the splintered bits of wood and the gleaming, shattered glass.

'You haven't touched anything, sir? Not picked up a brick or a stone?'

'Nothing,' said Neil, and Gran put in, 'That's what we were looking for. Vandals – you'd expect to find whatever they'd chucked.'

'You would,' agreed the policeman. 'Is there anyone else in the house?'

'No, just ourselves,' said Neil. 'We've only been here just over a week. My mother came up from London today.'

'And where were you when this happened?'

'Upstairs.' Neil explained about the flat, and the policeman wrote down the details.

'Were the outside doors locked, sir?'

'I'm afraid not.' Neil looked faintly embarrassed. 'Stupid, I suppose, but –'

'You'd think it would be all right here, though, wouldn't you?' Arabella put in. 'I mean, that's half the thing about not living in a town.'

'That's what people think,' said the policeman, still writing. 'Doesn't always work that way.' He glanced up and added, 'All right if we take a look round the rest of the house, sir?'

'Yes, of course. The electricity's on in most of it,' Neil said. 'It's just here and the downstairs corridor that's off.'

'How many people knew that besides yourselves?'

'Only the builders, I suppose.'

'And they are –?'

'Barkers. Two brothers.'

The policeman nodded. 'George and Arthur.' He buttoned his notebook into his pocket. 'Right, sir, we'll just check the other rooms.'

'I'll put the kettle on,' said Arabella.

Con was the last to leave the big, dark room. He paused and looked back at the wreckage of splintered glass and wood, hardly visible now as the moon vanished behind scudding clouds. He shivered, and not merely because of the cold wind that blew in through the smashed windows. *Careful*, the voice had said. But he had not been careful, there had seemed no need. Was it a crime to relax and enjoy yourself? If so, he'd rather not know.

In the kitchen, Gran was dropping tea-bags into the teapot, and Arabella sat at the table with her fringed shawl clutched round her shoulders, looking like a refugee. 'I know Neil just thinks I'm being stupid,' she said miserably.

'It's not that,' said Gran. 'Got a tea-cosy?'

'In the drawer. What is it, then? He hates me saying anything about what might be upsetting this house.'

'It scares him to death,' Gran said. 'Didn't you know that?'

'*Scares him?*' Arabella looked up, startled. 'But Neil's so sensible.'

'That's what he'd have you think. But he was the kid who couldn't listen to fairy-tales,' Gran went on. 'Mind you, they are quite scary. Hansel and Gretel getting fattened up so the witch could eat them, Red Riding Hood finding the wolf in bed, dressed up as her granny. I reckon they invented them to keep kids in order. But it was the same with telly. When Dr Who came on, Neil used to hide behind the sofa.'

'Poor Neil,' said Arabella. 'Poor darling.'

'He's not as tough as you think,' said Gran. 'Nice people never are. But he tries. Where's the sugar?'

'On the fridge, by those packets of herbal.'

Gran caught Con's eye. 'Cheer up,' she said. 'We're a good team, you and me. We'll get this place licked into shape.'

'Sure,' said Con. *As long as I'm careful.* From now on, he must never relax his guard.

Ten

Early the next morning, Con lifted his head from the pillow and listened. The house was full of noise – not just the wind, but hammering and sawing and the splintering of wood. He sat up sharply, and heard his parents' bedroom door open. Neil ran downstairs. Con pulled on his jeans and a sweater as voices rose from the big room below. Whatever was going on down there, he had to be part of it.

The house felt very cold. Summer had ended, and the rooms seemed full of the east wind that blew in through the empty frames downstairs.

'They're coming back this morning, to have a better look in daylight,' Neil was saying, 'so you mustn't clear up yet.'

'Weren't no business for the police,' Barker said. He had a stubby tenon-saw in his hand. 'Them frames been lousy with rot for years. When the wind got up last night, I said to Arthur, we best go and look at the Hall in the morning. Make sure that's all right.'

'He did,' agreed Arthur, leaning on his broom. A wheelbarrow stood on the parquet floor, already half full of glass.

'The survey didn't mention severe rot,' Neil argued. 'There was nothing to suggest this.' He swept an arm round the scene. It looked worse this morning, a bomb-site of shattered glass and wood.

Barker was unperturbed. 'You ask me, that's like teeth,' he said. 'Seem all right, then one morning you wake up with the toothache and you got trouble. Same with timber. The foundations go.' He picked up a broken piece of window frame and turned it in his freckled hands, then tossed it into the barrow. 'Rotten,' he said. Then he glanced at the terrace and added, 'Look like someone's up early.'

Gran came in. Her short grey hair was wind-blown, and she was wearing a track suit. 'Morning,' she said. Then she smiled at Barker and added, 'Destroying the evidence, are you?'

The builder glared at her. 'And what's that supposed to mean?' he demanded.

Arabella had come in, sleepy and dishevelled, tying the sash of her Japanese kimono, but nobody took any notice of her.

'What I say.' Gran was unruffled. 'Whatever there was for the cops to look at, you've sure as hell mucked it up.' Her Australian twang seemed stronger by contrast to Barker's Suffolk speech.

The creases in the builder's tweed jacket tightened as he pushed his thumbs into his belt, chin jutting in indignation. For a moment, he stared at Gran, and she stared back. Then he turned to Arthur and said, 'Right. Seems we int wanted.'

'Oh, but –' Arabella made a helpless gesture. 'Shouldn't we just –'

Barker turned to Neil. 'I put in a lot of work for you, Mr Smith,' he said. 'Give you some good advice as well, but there's none so deaf as what won't hear.' He looked at Arabella and went on, 'You best know the truth, missus, before you get any further. This place don't like you. Nor don't the village, neither. I dare say they'll come round in a year or two – people got short memories. But you won't never get the better of the Hall. A few broken windows is nothing. There'll be worse come to you than that.'

'Rubbish,' said Gran. But Arabella put her hands to her face with a kind of sob, then turned and ran from the room. In the silence that followed, everyone heard the blundering rush of her feet up the stairs and the slam of her bedroom door.

Neil turned to Barker and said with icy calm, 'That is deliberate scaremongering, and I won't have it. You may consider yourself finished with this job as from now, Mr Barker. I'll settle your account for the work done, but that's the end of it. You can collect your tools and go.'

Barker stared at him, and for the first time, Con thought the builder looked a little uncertain. 'No call to be like that,' he said.

'There is every call,' said Neil, 'and I have nothing further to say.'

Gran caught Con's eye from where she stood by the French windows, and gave him a small jerk of the head as she moved out on to the terrace. Con followed her.

'Best out of there,' she said. 'Leave 'em to it.'

In the walled garden, she stopped, looking round. 'Going to be great, this,' she said. 'I'll get it turned over this back end – maybe borrow a couple of pigs if there's anyone round here got them. Nothing like a pig for clearing the ground.'

'If we're still here,' Con said gloomily. 'Mum's really got the heebies now.'

'Of course we'll be here! Barker's done for himself, don't you see? He went too far, upsetting your mum like that. He'll never get us out now Neil's seen through his little game. Tell you what, though,' Gran went on, 'I had a good look at those windows this morning before Barker turned up, and I reckon he sabotaged them.'

'*Sabotaged*? What do you mean?'

'The frames still standing in the windows had been cut through. You could see they were freshly sawn. Keyhole saw, most likely, not to disturb the glass. Those two windows had been loosened, nothing holding them up. So the wind just blew them in. Can't prove it now, of course, he's mucked it all up.'

Con whistled. The sheer, calculated malevolence of it appalled him. But then he was struck by a new thought. 'At least Mum will know it wasn't a poltergeist. Just Barker.' That was almost as bad. 'But like you say, he's finished now, isn't he.'

Not quite. He means you harm.

The crow landed on the greenhouse roof with a squeak of claws on the green-mildewed glass. And Con shivered.

'Cold?' asked Gran.

'A bit.' And in truth, a chill had run down his spine as he realised that there was more to come. He wasn't clear of this business yet. The Bird Boy still had a use for him. Or Barker did.

The crow flapped away into the windy sky, and Con looked at his gran with a half-hearted grin. 'I was just kind of day-dreaming,' he said.

Gran didn't smile back. 'Be careful,' she said, as the crow had done – or whatever it was that spoke in Con's mind. 'Day-dreaming's fine, but it can creep up on you and get to be a habit, like fags and booze. Mind it doesn't get a hold on you.'

'I'll try,' said Con. And meant it.

The rest of the morning was full of rushing around. Neil went into a frenzy of telephoning, trying to find a new builder who had no connection with the Barkers. The police came again, but they didn't seem much interested in what Gran had to say about the window frames having been sawn through.

'Difficult to prove,' one of them said, turning a bit of broken wood in his hands as Barker had done. 'It's been freshly sawn, I'll give you that, but the site was being cleared, as you say. These saw-cuts could well have been made by Barker and his brother this morning, after the accident. And there certainly is some rot.' He looked at Neil and added, 'If you're claiming on your insurance, sir, it might be as well not to mention any question of sabotage.'

They took some photographs, then went away.

'Probably drinking pals of Barker's,' Neil said in the kitchen afterwards.

'Have you found another builder?' Arabella asked. She had cheered up a bit, but she still looked pale and startled, huddled in a huge jersey, her hair bundled all anyhow. She wasn't even wearing ear-rings.

'There's a guy from Diss called Marsh who sounds hopeful. He's playing football this afternoon, but he says he'll give us a look tomorrow. Nice of him to turn out on a Sunday.'

'Nice of us to give him the work,' said Gran, tough as ever. 'You got any sausages? I'm starving.'

That afternoon, Gran insisted on a bike ride, although Con simply wanted to curl up somewhere warm and think about being careful. The outside world seemed full of dangers. But Gran had looked at him and said, 'Come on. Fresh air is what you need.'

They pedalled up the long, slow hill to the water-tower, then went on, sometimes between hedges and sometimes skirting past open hedgeless fields, and went through villages that had patterns of round pebbles in the walls of their houses. Virginia creeper had turned scarlet against pink-washed plaster, and asters and dahlias bloomed in the gardens. They passed a huge church that stood in a clump of trees set in a green field, miles from anywhere else, and Gran shouted over her shoulder, 'Plague.'

'What?'

She coasted to a halt and put a foot down. 'There'd have been a village round it once,' she said, looking across at the church, 'only they got the plague. There was a lot of it here, I've been reading about it since we bought the Hall. It wiped whole villages out, and the few people left burned everything and started afresh a few miles away. Built new houses. Left the church – couldn't burn that anyway, being made of stone. Where are we?'

'I don't know,' Con confessed. 'I'm a bit lost.'

'That makes two of us,' said Gran. 'Never mind, there'll be a signpost or something.'

They went on past a couple of farms, then came to a large prefabricated building with large painted letters on it that said *Knockholt*.

'That's where Maggie's brother works,' Con said. 'Agricultural suppliers.'

'Don't tell me,' said Gran. 'Herbicides, pesticides. They'd write me off as all muck and magic, of course, but I'll show them. You can't grow decent stuff just on chemicals.'

They went on. A crackle of gun-fire sounded from behind some trees. Clay-shooting, Con thought. Maggie had explained about the things shaped like saucers that were flung into the air by a kind of catapult, to be shattered if you were a good enough shot. And he thought about Pete Barker, too. After what had happened, it would be all-out warfare with Pete. They came to a crossroads, and Con saw from the signpost they they'd come round in a wide circle.

'We're not far from home,' he said, with some relief. A thin rain was starting to blow in the wind.

As they came through the village, Gran stopped at the sight of the plants outside Mrs Fosdyke's shop. 'Hang on,' she said. She propped her bike against a tree and went to inspect the boxes of little green plants. 'Very nice. Someone knows what they're doing. I'll go and ask. You want a Coke or something?'

'I wouldn't mind,' said Con. *Mrs Fosdyke*. He prickled with fresh interest as he thought about this woman who had been the child of Annie Marsden. There hadn't been a chance to talk to her about it. Perhaps now was the time.

Now, now. And there was the crow, slithering rather absurdly among the slender branches of a cherry tree that bent under its weight.

You can just shut up, Con said to it. He was not in the mood for any more dark warnings. Enough was enough. He followed his gran into the shop.

The small group of people who had been gossiping beside the counter stopped talking as the two strangers came in. Their eyes followed Con as he went across to the upright fridge that had a handle shaped like a Coke bottle.

'Get me one as well,' his gran said, then turned cheerfully to the group and added, 'Nice drop of rain coming. We could do with that for the gardens.'

Nobody answered.

Con put his two cans on the counter.

'That be all?' asked Mrs Fosdyke.

'Yes, thank you.'

A man with a bristly black moustache said, 'Not buying a Lottery ticket, then?' and a couple of women giggled.

Gran dropped her change back in her pocket, passed one of the cans to Con and then, without hurry, opened the other one and took a swig. She wiped her mouth on the back of her hand and turned to face the man who had spoken.

'OK,' she said, 'so I won. Now, you tell me something. When you don't win, d'you reckon that's your fault?'

''Course not,' said the man. 'Int nobody's fault. Just luck.'

'Right,' Gran agreed. 'Both ways, it's just luck. So how about packing in the snotty comments?'

Nobody smiled. 'All very well, isn't it,' one woman said to another. 'Sitting on millions, and they come in here for no more'n a can of Coke. Don't do the village no good, do it?'

Con felt his face flush. This was not the time to talk to Mrs Fosdyke at all, it was awful. Everyone was jealous and resentful of him and his family. But Gran had leaned an elbow on the counter as if settling in to enjoy a good old argument. 'So you reckon I should be standing here handing out tenners, do you?' she said.

'Wouldn't come amiss,' said the man. One of the women nodded, but an older man was grinning.

Gran took another swig of Coke. 'Funny,' she said, surveying the black-moustached man calmly. 'I wouldn't have put you as the sort that asks for charity.'

'That I don't!' He was indignant. 'But there's sharing –'

'OK. What are you going to share with me?'

'*I* ain't won the Lottery.'

'But you could share a bit of friendliness. And if you had won,' Gran persisted, 'would you be handing me a tenner?'

'I might.'

This time, everyone laughed. 'He wouldn't give you his toenail clippings,' a woman said.

'Thing is,' Gran explained, 'it'll take all we've got and more to get the Hall up and running. After that, it'll be good for everyone, not just my family. There'll be jobs. House staff, cooks, gardeners – that's my pigeon, being as I'm a landscape gardener by trade. I'll need a fair bit of help.'

'Go on?' said Mrs Fosdyke from behind the counter. 'I might like that.'

All heads swivelled to look at her. It was as if a cat or a dog had spoken, the way they seemed so surprised.

Gran looked at her, too, but with a different kind of interest. 'Is it you who grew the plants outside?' she asked.

Mrs Fosdyke nodded, silent again.

'Got proper green fingers, she has,' said one of the women. 'You should see her garden. Carrots long as your arm, she grow.'

'Talk of gardens,' said the man with the moustache, 'I got to cut the lawn.' He gathered up his newspaper and packets of crisps, nodded at everyone, and went out.

'My lot will be wanting their tea.' The women drifted out as well, one or two of them giving Gran a smile. They weren't exactly friendly yet, but Con could see they were tickled by her straight way of talking. In another few moments, they had gone.

'Finished with these?' Mrs Fosdyke put the empty cans in a bin behind the counter.

Now, Conan. Now.

I can't, said Con.

Yes, you can. Go on.

He gave a little cough. 'Maggie Dew said your mother used to work at the Hall,' he ventured.

'Did she.' Mrs Fosdyke turned to tidy the already neat stacks of magazines.

Gran raised an interested eyebrow at Con. 'I'd like some of those wallflowers you've got outside,' she said to Mrs Fosdyke's back. 'Are they tall-growing or dwarf?'

'You best come and see – I got both.' Mrs Fosdyke lifted the flap of the counter and came out, ignoring Con.

Outside, Gran stared down at the boxes of plants, hands on her hips in a business-like way. 'Now, this could be quite a shipping order,' she said. Then she gave Con the ghost of a wink and went on casually, 'Will you nip home and ask your dad to bring the car down? If he's not too busy.'

You see? You see?

Con nodded. So he was to leave it to Gran.

He got on his bike and set off up the long, gentle hill, head down against the cold easterly wind, and the crow flapped steadily ahead of him. *Leading me home*, he thought.

Home, Conan. This is your home. And as Con looked up and saw the roofs of the Hall among its sheltering trees, he knew for the first time, with absolute certainty, that this was where he belonged.

When Neil had set off in the Volvo to collect Gran's

plants, Arabella sat down at the kitchen table, her hands heavy in her lap. She looked very tired.

'Shall I make you some tea?' Con asked.

'Please. Wild raspberry.'

He switched the kettle on, and urgent words spoke in his mind. *Tell her, Conan. Tell her now.*

All of it?

All of it.

He watched the deep pink colour flood into the mug of hot water. Yes, perhaps this was the time. It had been a blow to his mother to lose her faith in Barker, but it would be too harsh to let her think that her instinctive feeling about the Hall was totally wrong as well. He sat down at the table and folded his arms. Arabella was pressing the tea-bag with a spoon, staring unseeingly into the rising vapour. 'There's something I want to tell you,' Con said. 'About the Bird Boy.'

It took quite a long time.

Eleven

They were late to bed that night, because Arabella was full of what Con had told her, and the whole thing was endlessly talked over.

Neil couldn't accept the idea that Con was in touch with the Bird Boy. 'Come on,' he said, 'who are you kidding? All very well for Saint Joan, hearing voices – people believed in that stuff in those days. Whatever you heard, it was inside your own head. Of your own making.' He glanced at Arabella and added, 'Too much of the New Age voodoo, if you ask me.'

'It's not *my* fault!' Arabella protested. 'I didn't even know he was hearing things, he never said a word, did you, Con?'

'No. Not till now.'

'But you must admit, you were going on about all this being Meant,' Neil pointed out. 'Family connection, suicide, unquiet spirits. Fertile ground for a kid to build up fantasy, wasn't it?'

Arabella shrugged defensively. 'But all that's true,' she said.

'Don't know about the spirits,' Gran put in. 'Most of that was Barker's doing.'

Con felt deeply uncomfortable. All this argument didn't alter anything. It hardly mattered whether the words that came to him were of his own making. The fact was that they came – and so did the crow, a real, solid bird, capable of attacking Pete Barker and pinching his catapult. There was no point in trying to understand how it worked, or in trying to explain his feeling that it wasn't over yet. There was nothing he could do except wait for whatever would happen.

'Well, anyway,' Gran said, 'Flo Fosdyke thinks she's Meant to come and work here, being as her mum always promised they'd live in the Hall one day.'

'Why?' Neil looked astonished. Con hadn't got round to the bit about Mrs Fosdyke – he'd rather given up on all that.

'Her mother had been at the Hall before Flo was born,' Gran explained. 'General maid-of-all-work. But she had a thing going with Sebastian, Edwin's younger brother. He was Flo's father. They were going to get married, Flo says, only he was killed.'

Everyone nodded. They all knew now about the accident and the black horse. And the crow.

'Annie Marsden,' Con put in. 'Flo's mum.'

'Was that her name? Flo didn't say. Anyway,' Gran went on, 'this Annie thought she was going to be the lady of the manor. Went on thinking it for years, waiting for the lawyers to sort out all the stuff about the will – but it never happened, of course. So it'll be kind of odd, Flo working here as a gardener. She says she doesn't mind, though. 'Woont have wanted the running of a big place like that.' Gran's idea of a Suffolk accent was fairly comic, but nobody laughed.

'That's complete rubbish,' Neil said. 'Sebastian wasn't going to inherit the Hall. Edwin left it to his wife and then to the boy, Conan.'

'So weird, the same name,' Arabella said, not for the first time, but Neil ignored her.

'Seb might have been in with a chance to get the Hall if the boy had been known to be dead, but while there was a possibility he might still be alive, he hadn't a hope.'

'But what if Seb killed him?' Arabella was sparkling with excitement as this thought struck her. 'No, don't sigh, Neil. I mean it. Who's to say he didn't?'

'There'd be no point,' said Neil. 'If Seb was going to bump the kid off and inherit the Hall, he'd have to do it in some way that would stand inspection.

141

The body would have to be found, and the death would have to look like an accident. There'd be a post-mortem and an inquest, all the legal stuff.'

'Suppose so,' said Arabella with regret.

In the silence that followed, Con said silently, *Tell me what happened. Please*. But there was no reply. The air in the room seemed to be listening with him.

'I wonder,' said Gran. 'Flo said the last thing her mum saw of Mr Seb, he and Barker's grandfather were going off in the cart together, to the pub.'

Laughing.

'Laughing?' asked Con.

'I don't know,' said his gran.

'Off to celebrate,' Arabella said darkly.

Neil frowned at her and said, 'That's pure speculation.'

Something was bothering Con. 'But if they were going to the pub, wouldn't they have gone down the road?' he asked. 'I mean, it's in the village. So how did they end up by the pond? It's miles from the road.'

'Fifty years ago, the road to the village probably wasn't made up,' Neil pointed out. 'It would have been just a cart-track like the rest. And it's quicker to the village across the fields, as the crow flies.'

As the crow flies. Con almost smiled.

Gran had been thinking about it. 'If they killed the boy,' she said, 'they might have parked him somewhere while they went off to the pub, planning to come back and discover him. "Oh, goodness me, look what's happened. A nasty accident while we were down in the village, having a quiet pint with friends." Built-in abili.'

'Don't you start,' said Neil. 'Young Conan Fothergill probably decided he was fed up with the lot of them and took himself off. Changed his name, went abroad – who knows? If he was as dotty as people say, he wouldn't have known how to run the place anyway. The idea probably scared him stiff.'

'He wouldn't have done that,' Arabella protested. 'He couldn't. He was too strange. Too – fragile.'

Neil looked at his watch. 'I feel pretty fragile myself,' he said. 'And it's gone two in the morning. I'm off to bed.'

For Con, the night that followed was full of crazy dreams.

Four and twenty blackbirds, Mr Barker was saying. *Baked in a pie, as the crow flies.* The pockets of his tweed jacket were full of chaffinches that struggled and cheeped piteously, and he walked away across a vast field where small green plants grew to the horizon. Then he wasn't a man but a scarecrow, swinging in the wind on the single stick that supported him as his grinning turnip head said, again and again, *A nasty accident*. A woman ran along the field's edge, barefoot, her white nightie and her long hair flying with the ragged clouds. Two horses thundered behind her, their riders in the red coats of hunters, yelling and blowing horns. And somewhere in the dazzle of the sun, the Bird Boy soared in a crazy dance with a silver seagull, glinting and turning in the summer sky.

Con woke in panic. He was gasping for breath, and birdsong rang in his ears. He turned on his back and opened his eyes enough to see the grey light of dawn, then shut them again. Slowly, the thumping of his heart steadied.

No sky.

The voice that might be of his own making sounded thin and exhausted, as if it could not last much longer. Con waited, aware of the blood pulsing through his own living body.

No breath. They were too strong. And I was not a bird, I had no claws, no curving beak. I could not fly. I was in the cage. Dark, dark. They broke the silver chain.

Where is the cage? Con asked gently. His own silent words seemed loud and crude beside the fading voice.

There was a long pause, then – *There were horses.*

Hunting horses? For a moment, red coats filled Con's mind again, and a running woman. The question shrivelled away in silence.

This is the last day. You have been so good, Conan. Thank you.

The words were faint and remote, as if coming from a great distance. Con strained to hear more, and a last, barely audible message reached him.

Sleep well.

After that, the silence went on and on. Con stared into the pale dawn. *The last day*. Perhaps these were his last living hours, and in the coming day, he would die as the little chaffinch did. He gave a dry sob of terror, and burrowed into the soft darkness of his bed like a small animal in search of safety. Somewhere in the house, he heard the mobile phone ring and then stop. *Sleep well*. Amazingly, he slept.

It was late in the morning when he woke again, and a Sunday smell of big breakfast came drifting up the stairs. Gran had no truck with muesli and bananas – she liked a proper fry-up.

The kitchen seemed very peaceful. Neil and Arabella had the Sunday papers spread across the table, and Gran was mopping up the last of her tomato ketchup with a piece of bread. 'Hi,' she said as Con came in. 'Can I do you a greasy-spoon breakfast?'

'Yes, please,' said Con. His dawn waking was mingled now with a dream he didn't want to remember, and this real, warm kitchen was a comfort.

'They're free-range eggs,' said Arabella. 'Have you seen this about "Herbs on the Patio"? Such a nice idea.'

When Con was at the toast and marmalade stage, Gran said, 'So what's on for today?'

'Rest,' said Arabella. 'I don't want to do *anything*.'

'Barker's coming to pick up his stuff from the stable,' said Neil. 'Got his wife to phone at some unearthly hour of the morning.'

'Coward,' said Gran. 'He could at least have called you himself.'

'What time's he coming?' asked Arabella. 'I don't want to see him. I just feel so let down. I mean, I *trusted* him.'

'After lunch, his missus said, whatever that may mean. The new chap's coming as well,' Neil added. 'Better make sure we keep them apart. I'll see him in the office.'

'Flo Fosdyke's coming up to look at the garden,' Gran said. 'We need to make plans for the winter – and dig over some beds for the plants I bought.'

'I'm going to the farm,' Con said. 'To look at Maggie's kittens. It is all right to have one, isn't it?'

'Fine,' said Neil. 'It can go on the staff. Rodent control. I might get the VAT back on its Kit Kat.'

'Those are chocolate bars,' said Con.

'Well, you know what I mean,' Neil said. 'Don't be so pedantic. Is there any more coffee?'

'Lots,' said Arabella. She was wearing her jangling bracelets today, and looked much better.

The morning wandered gently on. Mrs Fosdyke turned up and went off across the yard with Gran, the pair of them nattering about the shortage of good horse manure, and Con set out for the farm. The new builder's van drove in as he left.

Birds joined him as he headed for the arch that led to the stable yard. This was ridiculous, Con thought. He was beginning to feel like that picture of St Francis they'd had at Albert Road, this brown-clad friar surrounded by birds while he told them about God. Only in Con's case, it was the birds who did the telling. They were crowding round him now, chivvying him towards the stable where Barker had his stuff.

'I'm not going in there,' he told them aloud. 'You've got it wrong. I'm going to the farm, to see Maggie.' But they became more insistent, circling round his head so closely that their wings almost brushed his face. He waved his arms, trying to clear a breathing space between them, and the panic of last night's dream was back. 'Oh, all *right*!' he said in desperation, and let them nudge him towards the stable door.

As soon as he stepped inside the shadowed building, the birds fell silent. Some of them came in with him, perching on the wooden partitions between the empty stalls, and others settled in the doorway or on the ground outside, a watching crowd.

From above Con's head, a new sound broke the silence. A battering of trapped wings, a tearing of frantic claws against wood, then a cry which sounded shatteringly loud – '*Caaa! Caaa!*'

Con gasped. So that was why the birds had brought him in. Somewhere up there above the wooden roof, the crow was trapped. He stared up into the dimness above the leaning shafts of the cart. There was no gap through which he could get into the loft space under the tiles, but he found himself gripping the dusty bars of the cart's sides, putting a foot on a wheel-spoke to lever himself up. The frantic squawking and fluttering went on over his head as he climbed on to the driving seat and stood upright, reaching for the wooden beams. Steadying himself with a hand on one of them, he pushed with the other at the planking of the ceiling – and a section of it shifted.

Con propped a foot on the heavy leather horse-collar that hung beside him on the wall, and pushed again with the palms of both hands. A square the size of a small trapdoor lifted clear, and he slid it sideways across the floor above him, then stared up into the dark space it had left. Fingers of daylight shone from gaps in the tiles, but he could see nothing.

'You can come out,' he said aloud. 'Look, this way.'

The crow hopped into view, black wings outspread, but it stayed where it was, hooked claws grasping the edge of the open trapdoor.

No, Conan. You must come up.

I can't, said Con.

You must.

Con's joints seemed to turn to water. *There were horses.* Was this the place the Bird Boy meant? Something waited for him up there, Con knew. Something that might cause his death. As it had done in the nightmare of dawn, a sob of terror gathered in his throat, but he put his hands on the edge of the trap beside the crow's grey claws, and pushed hard against the horse collar with one foot, the other swinging clear. His elbows were through the square hole, and he grappled for a handhold to pull himself up. His fingers met a gap in the floor's planking and he hauled himself forward, grovelling across the boards until he could get first one knee then the other on to the dusty surface.

The crow flew up on to the cross-beam. Still on all fours, Con stared up at it. Dust-motes drifted in the narrow shafts of light, and he saw that the place was very small, with no room to stand up except at the apex of the roof – but it seemed harmless. Apart from the old straw which was piled against the end wall, the loft was empty.

Suddenly, Con was aware that the key in his pocket was almost burning. He took it into his hand, bewildered – and the crow flew down and started tearing wildly at the straw, hurling beakfuls over its shoulder as it burrowed into it.

Quickly, Conan, quickly.

And at that moment, Barker's pick-up came into the yard. There was no mistaking that heavy engine and the rumble of its cross-country tyres. Doors slammed and voices sounded outside in the yard. Con knew he was trapped. Very quietly, he began to slide the square of wood over the hole, hoping to get it back into place before it was noticed.

He was too late. The doorway below him darkened with the bulky silhouette of Barker, followed by the smaller one of his brother. They came in, standing directly below him, and Con shrank back noiselessly from where he might be seen.

'You reckon we'd get away with it?' Arthur was saying.

'Won't get no trouble from the police,' said Barker. 'I got friends there, owe me a thing or two. I int letting this jumped-up Londoner get the better of me, boy, I tell you that.'

'He don't scare easy,' Arthur said gloomily. 'Them windows –'

'It's the old Aussie bird's the tough one,' said Barker. 'Been around, she has. Never you mind. She won't have much to yap about when the place go up in flames.'

'Shoulda done it in the first place,' Arthur grumbled, 'while we was still in the house. Int no bother to fix a short circuit, like I done in the bathroom. Now we got the push, it int so easy.'

'Who you kidding? Her with the ear-rings don't lock her doors, do she?' Con could hear the grin in Barker's voice as he went on in a parody of Arabella's London accent – "They're all so honest in the country".'

The crow was still tearing at the straw, careless of the loud rustling it made.

Shut up, Con said. *They'll hear you.*

And in that very minute, a silence fell in the stable below.

'Funny,' Barker said. 'I never seen that trap in the ceiling before.'

The crow did not stop. Its beak knocked on something hollow.

'Somebody up there,' said Arthur. He sounded panic-stricken. 'What'll we do?'

'Better not be,' Barker said grimly. 'I'll get a ladder.' He went out to the truck.

Quick, quick, quick.

Something was coming into view as the crow hurled more straw aside. A domed lid.

A hiding place, Con thought frantically. *Thank God.* The key was burning in his hand. He saw that the lid belonged to a small trunk. He hauled at it, but it didn't move. *The key.* It fitted easily into the corroded brass lock, and Con turned it and flung back the lid.

Then he froze.

Curled with its knees to its chest lay a skeleton, its thin bones white in the dim light. The fragile skull was bent towards the hands, and hanging across the slender arch of a rib was a fine silver chain, its broken ends dropping into the empty darkness that had once been a boy. Lying within the delicate bones of the curled fingers was a small, finely-wrought thing that took the last of Con's breath away as he stared at it, for a pencil of sunlight shone on the neat head and spread wings of a silver seagull.

'Now we'll see,' said Barker from below him. The top of a ladder appeared at the trap, and heavy footsteps began to come up.

Very gently, Con closed the lid of the trunk. *The last day*. So this was the end. With strange calm, he turned to face the man whose bulk filled the square hole of the trap. A powerful torch-beam shone in his eyes, and he put his arm across his face to check the glare.

'Well, well,' said Barker. 'Doing a little eavesdropping, was you.' He reached a hand across the floor and levered himself further into the loft. 'You, sunshine, are going to have a nasty accident.'

Con put both hands over his face, and wordlessly prayed.

The answer came as a mad bleating from below, followed by a yell from Maggie.

'Con! You up there? Are you all right?'

Barker's hand had been within an inch of Con's ankle, but it paused as the builder swore under his breath. And Con screamed back, 'GET HELP, QUICK!' It was so loud that he felt as if his throat would split.

Barker retreated down the ladder, shouting

something at Arthur – then plunged out of sight in a splintering of dry wood.

For a long moment, Con could not move. Dust rose in the silence. He crept to the edge of the trapdoor and stared down. Barker lay sprawled among the broken bars of the cart's side, the ladder at an angle beneath him. His face was turned upwards, but he didn't seem to see Con. A tweed-clad arm dangled, and his right leg was twisted under him in a way that didn't seem natural. And Arthur – Con wondered if he was dreaming – was backing away from a white goat which was nibbling experimentally at his Fair Isle sweater. There was no sign of Maggie. Gone for help.

Con began to laugh, then found he was almost in tears. The Bird Boy. Conan, his namesake. The little skeleton.

Arthur flailed his arms at the goat, which put the top of its head down and butted him in the ribs.

'*William!* Stop that!' Maggie shouted, appearing in the doorway with Gran and Mrs Fosdyke behind her, both of whom were panting a bit.

Gran walked past Arthur and the goat and ignored the spread-eagled man in the cart, though he was now groaning. She looked up at Con and asked, 'You all right?'

'Yes,' said Con. But his legs felt so shaky that he

wondered how he was ever going to get down from the loft.

'More than this one is,' Gran said, turning to inspect Mr Barker. 'Hospital case, by the look of him. Flo, could you go up to the house, tell them what's happened? Get Neil to phone for an ambulance.'

Mrs Fosdyke nodded and moved off – but at the door she looked back and burst out, 'He want to be in a Black Maria, not an ambulance. That boy scream like a rabbit with a stoat, heard him right from the kitchen garden, yelling for help. Didn't know where it was, then Maggie come running like all the devils in hell were after her. Funny goings-on, if you ask me.' And she went out, muttering.

Maggie had got hold of the rope that dangled from the goat's collar. She looked up at Con and said, 'The crow came to get me.'

'The *crow*?' But surely the crow was here? Con looked round the dim loft, at its rafters and scattered straw and the small trunk that stood with its lid closed. The crow was utterly absent.

'You don't want to take no notice of Flo Fosdyke.' Arthur suddenly unleashed a torrent of words. 'Everyone know she got funny ideas. The lad got hisself stuck up there, climbed up and couldn't get down, that's always harder coming down. So George said he'd get a ladder off the truck, help him, like. Ladder weren't much of a length, so he put it on the cart and held it. Then this darn goat come in, butt me up the backside. Let go the ladder, didn't I.' He looked at his sprawled brother and added, 'That's what he get for being good-hearted.'

'It isn't true,' Con said furiously from the loft. 'You were planning to burn the Hall down, I heard you. And Mr Barker said I was going to have an accident.' *A nasty accident*. But even as he spoke, Con knew how feeble his words sounded.

'As well you might,' Arthur agreed. 'He were worried in case you fall, boy. And as to the rest of it, you heard wrong. Or else you was dreaming.'

For a moment, Con looked down into the foxy brown eyes, then he smiled. *It's all right*, he thought. *The Hall is safe now*. It was all over. He could have put his head down on his arms as he lay there on the dusty floor of the loft, and slept in utter peace beside the small trunk amid its straw. In this strange moment, before time moved on and led to the telling of the tale, he was the only person who knew of the curled form that lay in the warmth of the key's unlocking. No voice spoke in his quiet mind. There was no fear and no yearning. It was perfect.

Twelve

After that, of course, chaos broke out. Barker was carted off to the hospital, and the ambulance men said he had concussion and a badly broken leg, and probably cracked ribs as well.

'Good,' Arabella said viciously. 'I wish he'd broken his neck. If it hadn't been for Maggie and her goat, Con would be dead.'

'I must admit, I feel rather the same,' said Neil.

The police arrived, bringing a lot of experts with them. This was very different from yesterday's visit and the rather casual glancing round at the wrecked windows, Con noticed. These men were full of importance over what they called Human Remains. He wished they didn't have to go into the loft with their lights and cameras and all the paraphernalia of their forensic stuff. But perhaps the Bird Boy wouldn't mind. He was free now that his body had been found and the truth could be guessed at. Perhaps he was flying in the sky with his seagull mother, or mingling with the sun and the clouds. Those who were still living could imagine what they liked.

In the new quietness, Con felt oddly alone, as if a part of himself had left him. Arabella had said once that when Con was born, she missed having him inside her, even though the last days of pregnancy had been so burdened and awful that she'd wanted them to end. 'You'd turned into your own self,' she explained. 'Magical and marvellous, but not part of me any more.' Con knew now exactly how she'd felt.

A young woman drove up just as the police were leaving.

'Hi,' she said, 'I'm from the *East Anglian Daily Times*. Are you Conrad?'

'Conan,' said Con.

'Great.' She switched on a small tape-recorder. 'And how did you feel, Conan, when you found the skeleton?'

Neil came to the rescue. 'All right, Con, I'll deal with this. You go in the house.'

And Con went.

That evening, Arabella had to lock all the doors against the press people who tramped about in the garden, taking photographs, and shouted through the letter-box with requests for interviews.

'Good thing I didn't put Flo's plants in,' said Gran. 'They'd have been squashed flat.'

'It's worse than when you won the Lottery,' said Con.

'Much worse,' Neil agreed. 'And it'll go on longer. Whatever you do, Con, don't breathe a word about this Bird Boy business, or you'll be stuck with it for the rest of your life. *The Boy Who Spoke to Spirits. My Friend Was a Ghost.* In all the papers, on TV. You'd never live it down.'

'Too right,' said Con. It was bad enough already, with Pete and his gang flapping imaginary wings and yelling, 'Bird Boy! Loony!' But there probably wouldn't be much of that from now on, once the news got round about what Barker had been up to. 'We'd better warn Maggie, though,' he added.

Neil groaned. 'Don't tell me she's in it as well?'

'Sort of. I mean, she turned up at the stable because the crow fetched her. She was taking the goat for a walk, and the crow came diving down, flying all round her and cawing. It wouldn't let her go anywhere else.'

'I don't want to know,' said Neil. He handed Con the phone. 'Have a word with her – tell her she mustn't talk to the press.'

'What's the number?'

'Hang on, I've got it in my notebook.' Neil fished

out his electronic organiser and began pressing buttons. He glanced up and added, 'Make it two kittens, by the way.'

'*Two?* Oh, great!' But Con was surprised. What had caused this sudden generosity?

'The new builder had a look in the attic,' Neil said with a slightly sheepish grin, 'to see about the scuttering noise. And it's mice.'

Neil drove Con to school the next morning, the car's windows tightly shut against a reporter who ran alongside. They stopped to pick up Maggie at the top of the lane.

'Barker broke his leg in three places,' she said. '*And* got broken ribs. My auntie's a nurse at the hospital.'

Nobody answered. It didn't seem to matter much now.

'What'll happen next?' Maggie asked. 'Will he go to prison for trying to burn the Hall down?'

'No,' said Neil. 'He didn't actually do anything. We can't even prove he sabotaged the windows.'

Con frowned. 'But I heard him and Arthur saying –'

'I know you did,' said Neil. 'But the point is, it's your word against theirs. And we have to face the fact that no actual crime was committed. I feel like you do, but the law's the law.'

Con watched the fields go by. There was nothing to say.

Pete Barker wasn't at school. Two or three of his henchmen stood about, looking sulky, but nobody took any notice of them. Everyone had heard about what happened, and Con was surrounded by an excited crowd. He'd just been exploring, he told them, and came across this chest in the attic, that was all. Maggie watched him shrewdly and said nothing.

'Where's your crow?' Jan asked.

'I don't know,' said Con. Since climbing down from the loft on the ladder which Neil held so carefully, he had not seen a sign of the crow. Perhaps it had gone to join the Bird Boy, he thought. Wherever that might be.

It turned out to be quite a good day. Con got into an impromptu football game during dinner break, and scored a cracking goal between the two school bags that stood for posts. Lots of people thumped him on the back, and the PE master, who had been watching, offered him a trial for the school team.

Lessons were more or less a write-off, as usual. There was too much to think about. 'Conan,' he heard Miss Ainsworth say at one point, 'I know you've had a rather dramatic weekend, but could you pay just a little attention?'

'Sorry,' said Con. And several people smiled at him as if they were old friends.

Arabella was singing as she painted the wall in the room she was going to use for aromatherapy and massage.

'Someone gave her a pot of jam,' said Gran. 'Cheered her up no end. And asked her to give a talk to the Women's Institute.'

'Oh, good,' said Con. 'I'm going over to the farm, to see the kittens. D'you want to come? Help me choose.'

On their way, they stopped and looked at the pond.

'Neil wants to fill it in,' said Con.

His gran looked at him, understanding what he'd left unsaid. 'But you'd rather keep it?'

Con nodded.

His gran stared down at the green water and the half-submerged junk. 'History doesn't go away just because you bury it,' she said. 'We know what happened here. It's just a question of what to do about it. Don't know what you think, but I'd like to turn it into a garden. Nothing formal, I don't mean like a park, with beds of salvias. But if we had a weeping ash at the top of the slope, and wild iris down by the water . . . clear some of these brambles and level the approach to the pond a bit, put stone steps in.' She had her hands on her hips, surveying the site. 'It could be a place where your mum's Yoga people could come and meditate.'

'She'd like that,' said Con. And so would the Bird Boy. When the police and the museum people and everyone else had finished whatever they were doing, they would bring him back here. This was where those frail bones should lie, out here on the hill beside his seagull mother.

It was a quiet autumn day when they buried the Bird Boy. People came from the village, dozens of them. Con suspected it was because Neil had promised a buffet lunch at the Hall afterwards, but they wore dark clothes and stood in respectful silence, some of them with bunches of dahlias and Michaelmas daisies from their gardens. Their eyes took in the stone slab and newly-upright headstone where Larina lay. Beside it, the new grave waited, its earth in a tidy pile nearby, covered with a green cloth made of artificial grass. The brambles on this side of the pond had gone, and stone steps led down to the water in a gentle curve. Gran had planted her weeping ash tree at the top of the slope where she had said, and its slender branches hung all round it like an almost-bare maypole, shedding yellow leaves.

Con felt as if he was dreaming. Maggie stood beside him, but she was wearing a skirt and black tights and a black jacket with a fluffy fur collar that looked as if it belonged to her mother. Neil was talking to the vicar, a tall, white-haired man in black robes and purple stole, holding a big, leather-bound Bible that had a white silk marker hanging from it. Mrs Fosdyke wore a new black hat with no feathers, and her ankles bulged a little over uncomfortable-looking black shoes. Arabella was in a long black dress, with a crocheted shawl hugged round her shoulders. She'd bought it the previous week at a Craft Fair, and its mad patchwork of crimson and violet, black and brown brought a few sideways glances from the silent crowd.

The gleaming black car with windows along its sides came slowly up the track, and men went to meet it, Neil and Allan Dew among them. Maggie whispered that the tubby man with a red face was Mrs Fosdyke's husband, and Con recognised another face as well – the man with the black moustache who had been in the shop that day when he'd gone in with Gran. Gran herself, amazingly neat in a dark grey jacket and trousers, saw him, too, and raised her eyebrows at Con.

Wreaths of flowers were brought out and laid on the grass. Somehow, Con had expected that the Bird Boy would still be in the small trunk with a domed lid, but the men had taken a pale, narrow coffin on to their shoulders and were bringing it down the grassy slope. *Yes*, Con thought in sudden relief. *I'm glad it's not the trunk.* He wondered where it was. *We should burn it*, his mind ran on. *I don't want that thing to exist any more.* Clean flames, out here on the hill.

The words the vicar spoke flew away into the sky that was the colour of Michaelmas daisies, and Con could not grasp their meaning. Then the men lowered the coffin into the grave, paying out the white ropes carefully, and the vicar stooped for a handful of earth. Con stared down at his feet in their cleanest trainers. *It's all right*, he thought fiercely, *he's free now. It's what he wanted.* Maggie did not look at him, but she slipped her hand into his.

It was only afterwards, when the people were streaming away down the track to the Hall, that the birds came. They swirled in a great spiral above the pond and its willow trees then circled round Con, who still stood by the grave with Maggie at his side. He didn't like crowds much – they either fussed and asked questions or they left you wondering if you ought to find something to say, and if so, what.

165

Maggie squinted up at the birds. 'They seem agitated,' she said.

'Yes.' Con stared up as well, shading his eyes from the autumn sun. A second wave of birds was whistling through the sky, bigger ones, ragged and untidy. Crows.

They settled in the trees and on the grass, and were suddenly silent, a congregation as dark and watchful as the people had been. Their quietness was charged with a kind of meaning, as though they, too, were waiting for an event. Their heads were all turned one way, towards the little weeping ash tree that Con's gran had planted.

'There's something up there,' Maggie said.

Con was already walking up the slope. Tears were gathering in a great ache. He saw the neat, black shape lying on the grass by the trunk of the young tree, and knelt beside it.

'Oh, no,' said Maggie.

Con stroked the folded wings with a gentle finger, and his tears overflowed. A half-moon of blue showed under the closed eyelids, and the iron-grey claws lay in a loose clasp of nothing. He picked the bird up and got to his feet.

Maggie joined him. She parted the crow's breast feathers with a careful finger, exploring. 'That's not been shot,' she said, 'There int a mark on him.' And

166

Con remembered what she had told Pete. *That int going to die until it chooses*. He rubbed his eyes on his sleeve. *A good bird*. But this had been more than a bird. The crow had, for a while, been part of his own self.

'I'll bury him for you, if you like,' Maggie offered, though her eyes, too, were welling with tears.

Con shook his head. When he knew he could speak steadily, he said, 'We'll have a fire. Clean everything.' The crow belonged in the sky, like cloud and smoke and sunshine. In every way that mattered, it was there already.

Maggie looked up at him helpfully. 'Your gran was saying she got a lot of woody stuff,' she said. And as Con met her concerned gaze, he made a little sound that was almost a laugh. She was so practical. 'Yes,' he said.

As they set out for the Hall, the crowd of birds flew up with a rush of wings and a wild twittering of what sounded like happiness. They circled once and then streamed away across the fields – all except for one. As Con carried the dead bird, he was aware of a presence above him, and looked up to see a black crow flying steadily above him and Maggie, close enough for the rush of air through its wing feathers to sound as a muffled whistle. It flew with them all the way along the track to the Hall.

As they came into the kitchen yard, Con thought of that first day when Maggie had been sitting on the wall. He had a moment's anxiety, remembering how she had refused to set foot in the house. 'You are coming in, aren't you?' he asked.

Maggie smiled. 'I reckon,' she said.

The crow that had flown with them lifted higher, parting company, and Con knew that it would send him no words to blossom within his own thoughts.

'*Caaa!*' the crow called, in the language of all crows. '*Caaa! Caaa!*' And Con did not mind when it soared away into the clear autumn sky.